Praise for
SUSAN SHREVE'S
Ghost Cats

Other Signature Titles

Jonah, the Whale and How He
Became Incredibly Famous
Susan Shreve

Bad Girls
Cynthia Voigt

Bat 6
Virginia Euwer Wolff

P.S. Longer Letter Later
Ann M. Martin and Paula Danziger

The Music of Dolphins
Karen Hesse

Out of the Dust
Karen Hesse

Ghost Cats

*

*

by Susan Shreve

*

SCHOLASTIC
Signature

an imprint of
Scholastic Inc.

New York Toronto London Auckland Sydney
Mexico City New Delhi Hong Kong

ISBN 0-439-26100-7

Copyright © 1999 by Susan Shreve.
All rights reserved.
Published by Scholastic Inc. SCHOLASTIC, the LANTERN logo, and associated logos are trademarks and/or registered trademarks of Scholastic Inc.

12 11 10 9 8 7 6 5 4 3 2 1   0 1 2 3 4 5/0

Printed in the U.S.A.   40

First Scholastic paperback printing, October 2000

Original hardcover edition designed by Elizabeth Parisi, published by Arthur A. Levine Books, an imprint of Scholastic Press, September 1999

* *Also by Susan Shreve* *

JONAH, THE WHALE
AND HOW HE BECAME
INCREDIBLY FAMOUS

For Po

Contents

May ********************* 1

September **************** 25

October **************** 51

November *************** 69

December *************** 87

January *************** 103

February************** 121

March *************** 131

April *************** 145

May *************** 155

Ghost Cats

May

*

*

Yesterday after school, I walked home in a terrible storm. I let myself in the front door of our town house in Boston, turned on the light in the hall because the rain had darkened the day to almost evening, and there under the round table where the mail is kept, was my ten-year-old cat, Rrrr. He was dead.

I could tell immediately. The way he lay stretched out, his head flung back, the way his legs had stiffened, his absolute stillness, his half-opened eyes.

I had seen dead before and more than once.

I walked upstairs, went into my room, closed the door, and sat on the bottom deck of my new double-decker bed. I probably sat there, straight up with my feet on the floor, for quite a long time, wondering if I too might die because my heart was beating so fast. I was hoping someone would come home so I didn't have to spend the afternoon sitting alone on my bed with Rrrr downstairs under the table. But no one did, and no one would until five o'clock when my mother finished at her law school and picked up Susanna. Susanna had a play-date as usual, with one of her trillion new best friends in kindergarten, and I didn't know where Emily, my other sister, was going after school, of course. I never did. In the last month, she had started liking boys. My brother Tobias had stayed after school because he has to have tutoring for his learning disability, which is something he didn't have until we moved to Boston this year. That's the trouble with Boston. All kinds of unexpected things have happened since we arrived here.

Before we moved to Boston, we were always together, the four of us, a regular team of children — a "domestic army" my father likes to say.

∗ ∗ ∗

My father is a pediatric neurologist and knows some information about children's brains that is valuable to doctors in other countries. That is the way my mother has explained his job to us. So, every year or two, we move to a new city, rent a house full of someone else's furniture near the hospital where my father will be teaching and start a new school — sometimes in the middle of the year.

I liked this life. I looked forward to the evening when my father would announce at dinner, "We're moving again."

Always the conversation was the same.

"Where now?" we'd ask.

He'd fold his hands on the table, smile in that secretive way he has, his lips closed, curling up like question marks.

"Guess," he'd say.

"The United States?" Emily asked.

He shook his head.

"Johannesburg?" I asked.

"Back to Edinburgh, I hope," Tobias said. "That was my very favorite."

"Belly, belly, Alaska," Susanna giggled. "I want to live in Belly, belly for the rest of my life."

"Maybe next time it'll be Belly, belly, Alaska," my father said. "But this time it's Tokyo."

Tokyo is the last place we lived before we moved to Boston.

"In Tokyo we'll live in a two-bedroom apartment and all of you will share one room," my mother said.

That night we sat on our parents' bed in Rome, which was where we were living at the time, while my mother read from the guidebook about Tokyo. And then we pretended we were Japanese children, sitting on cushions on the floor, whispering in our made-up Japanese and drinking hot tea.

We never had time in any city to make friends. Besides, our lives were too exciting.

I loved it when we moved. I especially liked the moment when we got to the airport of the city we were leaving with our passports and bookbags, walked down the long windowless corridor to the entrance of the plane, and flew over the world to our new home.

Usually we sat in the middle aisle of a jumbo jet, six across — my parents at either end, halfway back so we could see the movie. I never slept on the plane. I read the guidebooks imagining our next lives. On the trip to Tokyo, I was particularly excited because we'd never been to Asia.

One Christmas, our parents had given us a map so we could color in bright red the places we had lived and watch the spread of red on our map each time we moved. By the time we moved to Japan, most of the map of the world had a splash of red and now we'd be able to make our red mark on Asia.

∗ ∗ ∗

For as long as I can remember, my father has called us a "domestic army," but I didn't know exactly what that meant until we arrived in Tokyo and I asked my mother that first night as we were unpacking our suitcases in our new apartment.

"So here we are in Tokyo," my mother said. "And we don't know anyone in Japan and you don't know anyone in your new school."

(That was the year Tobias was saying "right on" in the middle of every conversation.)

"Most kids would be worried," Mother said.

"Not us," Emily said, climbing into her new bed.

"Are you worried, Peter?" my mother asked.

"I love it," I said.

"Me too," Susanna said.

"Tobias?"

"I like everything Peter likes."

"So why is it that you're not worried about being in this strange place where you don't have any friends and don't speak the language?" Mother asked.

"Because we're best friends with each other," Emily said.

"Exactly. And that's what makes you a domestic army," my mother said. "A team."

I was nine when we moved to Tokyo and I think

I was happier there than any place we had lived before. We were in one bedroom with four beds lined up against the wall like a dormitory, and at night when the lights were out in our room, we whispered back and forth until one by one we fell asleep. I was always the last to fall asleep, listening to the others breathing.

The trouble with happiness is that you don't really know you have it until it's gone.

✳ ✳ ✳

This morning when I left for school, Rrrr was in perfect health as usual, eating his dry Meow Mix, lying down in front of his bowl as he liked to do, cleaning his paws when he had finished. I picked him up, kissed him on the lips because my mother thinks it's disgusting to kiss a cat on the lips, and left for school with my brother, Tobias. Tobias was crying, as he often does now because he hates school now that he has learning disabilities. He's seven and too old to cry about going to school, but that makes no difference to Tobias. And I don't blame him because at the American School in Tokyo, he was smart but by the time we got to Boston, he wasn't smart any longer.

People have always known us as the Hall kids and we're well known in all the places we have lived — four-strong and "thick as thieves" as my mother likes to say. Which means stuck together, locked in place like LEGO blocks.

We have moved every year or so since I was three. From Ghana in West Africa to Prague, Czechoslovakia, to Washington, D.C., to Houston, Texas, to Edinburgh, Scotland, to Rome, Italy, to Tokyo, Japan, and finally to here, Boston, Massachusetts.

I don't remember Ghana but I've seen pictures of me in a straw hat and short pants, without a shirt — usually carrying a stuffed zebra. There are hundreds of pictures of me in the markets, sitting on someone's lap, walking along the dusty streets holding my mother's hand, at my father's hospital peering into a wooden box at a newborn baby, or wandering down a dirt road full of chickens and dogs and women in their bright-colored clothes carrying water on their heads.

In Prague we lived in an apartment in the old city and what I remember especially was the Powder Tower of the Prague Castle, where gunpowder used to be stored. I also loved to walk through the crowds of people and acrobats and musicians across the Charles Bridge spanning the Vltava River. Emily and I used to say "Vltava" over and over pretending we could speak Czech.

"Vltava czovech ouchie," I'd say to Emily on our way to school.

"Vltava, vlatava, non non ouchie blec," she'd reply.

At night my father would tell us stories of how it had been in Prague before the Velvet Revolution in 1989, the year after I was born, when the communists, who had been ruling Czechoslovakia, lost power and the Czech people were free. The revolution was called "velvet" because there was no bloodshed. Although I was only five when we left Prague, I remember standing in the apartment with its huge windows overlooking the square, pretending to watch the Velvet Revolution.

When we moved from Prague to Washington,

D.C., and unpacked our suitcases and chose our rooms — Tobias with me, Emily alone, Susanna in a bassinet with my parents — my mother said we would live in Washington for a very long time.

"How do you know?" I asked her with a sinking feeling.

"Because your father loves his job at Children's Hospital and he's promised me we can stay for quite a while."

I shrugged.

"Of course he may be *needed* in a poorer country where they don't have doctors for children's brains," I said.

"He's also needed here, where there are quite enough poor children to fill his time," she said. "So I hope we stay."

* * *

In Washington, my mother and I used to walk around the neighborhoods looking at houses she might like to buy.

"Do you like that house, Peter?" she'd ask, pointing to one house or another.

I had very little interest in the look of houses, but during the time that we lived in Washington I was beginning to understand that my mother was in love with houses and wanted one of her very own. That she didn't like moving as much as I did.

One warm afternoon during a long walk with Susanna in a stroller, my mother took me to a house she had discovered in a neighborhood with children running up and down the streets and a playground and a large brick elementary school with LAFAYETTE over the front doors. The house was large and yellow with black shutters and a large front porch with a FOR SALE sign in the front yard.

"What do you think?" she asked me.

"I could probably have my own room?" I asked.

"Of course you could," my mother said.

"Are we going to buy it?" I asked, hoping to stall the conversation. I certainly didn't want to buy a house. If we bought one instead of renting as we always had, then we'd have to live in it for a long time.

"Maybe," she had replied, squeezing my shoulder, kissing the top of my head, as if we were conspirators.

But she was wrong. Already, my father had made plans to leave.

* * *

When Susanna was three months old, we moved from the rented house in Washington, D.C., before we had even had a chance to visit the zoo or the Smithsonian or the White House, to another rented house in Houston, Texas,

The whole time we lived in Houston on Georgetown Road where my father was teaching at the University of Texas Medical Center, my mother was in a bad humor.

Sometimes, in Houston, she didn't even get dressed until lunch. It was summer, oven-hot, the streets empty of children, and she'd wear her floating white nightgown while we played board games at the kitchen table or else "Pretend Family."

Pretend Family is a game my mother made up and is her personal favorite. In the Pretend Family, there are four children — we use carrots to play the roles of the children — and a mother and a father who are represented by eggplants. They all live in a beautiful house on Bolero Street in Love City, Rhode Island, and the children go to Better-than-Ever Elementary School. Pretend Family has never traveled further away than the suburbs of Love City — except to visit their grandparents, who live at the beach.

"I want to live in one house for the rest of my life," my mother told me one afternoon while we were having tea and cookies. "Then you children will have a chance to make good friends who invite you to birthdays and sleepovers. I can go to law school, and we can throw away the suitcases forever."

One night in Houston, in the room I shared with Tobias, next door to our parents' bedroom, I overheard an argument between them. My father didn't raise his voice but my mother did, and what I heard her say in a high-pitched, teary voice filled me with fear.

"This is the last time I'll move any place," she said. "Next time you go alone."

After that, I couldn't fall asleep.

"So I guess we're going to be in Houston for a long time," I said the next morning as we walked to school with my mother with Susanna in her stroller.

"Not me," Tobias said. "I don't like my teacher."

"Well, I'm going to stay," Emily said. "I have a new friend called Mari Sue and she has a swimming pool and she invited me to the beach."

"Great," I said. " I think I'll go to Paris."

We always walked to school along a route that crossed a footbridge over a bayou where Emily was convinced she had seen rats swimming. So on the bridge, we'd stop, lean over the railing, and look down at the gray-green slimy water searching for rats.

"I see one," Emily would screech.

"I see six," Tobias would say. "One mother and five babies."

My mother would assume a creepy voice, very low and gravelly, singing, "I dreamed I was in rat's alley, where the dead men lost their bones."

✳ ✳ ✳

That morning my mother didn't stop at the bridge as we walked over the bayou.

"Aren't we going to look for rats?" Emily asked.

"Not today," my mother said.

"We always look for rats," Tobias said.

My mother didn't reply.

At recess, Emily came over to me on the playground to ask what in the world was the matter with our mother.

"I think she's tired of moving," I said.

"Me too," Emily said. "I'd like to stay in Houston with Mari Sue."

"But that's not going to happen," I said, in quite a terrible mood. "Daddy'll be asked to go to a new hospital soon, so get over it."

That afternoon when I got home, I noticed that my mother had a catalogue from the University of Houston Law School opened on the kitchen table.

"So you're going to law school?" I asked.

"I don't know yet," she said. "I just wanted to find out the requirements to apply."

At first, law school sounded fine. I pictured my mother attending school in a building next to our school. We'd walk to school with her in the morning and wait for her in the afternoon. At night, we'd all sit at the kitchen table doing our homework — even my father, who works on his scientific projects after dinner. I had no idea at the time that teachers at law schools (at least the one in Boston where my mother is now in school) would have no interest in the fact that she has children and would expect her to study day and night.

"Maybe we'll stay in Houston and you can go to law school here," I said.

"Maybe," my mother replied, but she didn't seem optimistic.

✳ ✳ ✳

Just after Susanna learned to walk, my father came home with the news that we were moving to Edinburgh, Scotland, where there was a splendid castle at the end of a long walk called The Royal Mile. After that, we moved to Rome, and then to Tokyo, and finally to Boston, Massachusetts. My mother says we will certainly live here for the rest of our lives — in this same brownstone house with a square garden in the back and a high stockade fence covered with ivy.

Since we have never lived any place long enough to make real friends until this year, it isn't difficult to understand why we are "glued together," our own best friends, except for the cats.

* * *

Before any of us was born but me, we had two cats. There was my father's cat, Martha Washington, a fat, short-haired cat with half a tail and mismatched eyes, and my mother's cat, Glimmer, a failed Persian with a skinny body and a fluffy tail. Glimmer and Martha were born in Paris, where I was also born. My cat Rrrr, a striped tabby whose name matched his meow, was born in Accra, Ghana, in West Africa. I got Rrrr when I was two years old so I would have a friend. That was my mother's idea.

"Peter's pal" is how my mother referred to Rrrr so I wouldn't be jealous of Emily when she was born. As it turned out, I wasn't jealous of Emily. I was perfectly happy to have an actual child spend the night and be there at breakfast in the morning and stay all day.

"Rrrr" came by his name naturally. He was interested in human beings but he didn't like to be particularly close to them, except for me. If anyone tried to touch him, he would make a long, sad growly sound that came out of his mouth as "Rrrrrrrrrrrr."

We began to have long conversations back and forth.

"Rrrr," he would say.

"Rrrrrr," I replied.

"Rrrrrrr," he continued. "Rrrrrrrrrrrrrrrrr."

We could talk on and on for a very long time.

✳ ✳ ✳

When Emily was two, we were living in Prague and she got to have her very own kitten because of Tobias. Not only was Tobias about to be born, but my mother was also going to Paris in order to have him at the American Hospital there. So Emily and I were left for two weeks in the care of an unpleasant woman we called "Onion" for how she smelled — Miss Onion-Bunion was actually the name we gave her. And Emily was given Jabberwock, a small, yellow-and-white brain-damaged kitten with a cockeyed smile to make up for Mother leaving in the first place and then returning with a new baby.

For months, Jabberwock didn't have a name at all except Yellow Cat. Until one day.

"Here Yellow Cat, Yellow Cat," my father called.

And Emily fell on her stomach, kicking her legs in the air and screaming.

"Her name isn't Yellow Cat."

"Then you'll have to give her a name, darling," my father said.

"Why not Fluffy?" my mother asked.

"Because I hate the name Fluffy," Emily said.

"What about Ebenezer?" my father asked.

"Or Velvet Revolution in honor of Prague," I suggested.

"Or just Velvet in honor of her soft, yellow fur," my father suggested.

"No," Emily said. "Those are all stupid names."

"What about Jabberwocky from *Alice in Wonderland*?" I asked.

"I don't like *Alice in Wonderland*. It doesn't make sense."

But I began to notice Emily walking around the apartment in Prague with Jabberwock under her arm, whispering, "Nice Jabberwock. Sweet baby Jabberwock." The next time my father called, "Here Yellow Cat," Emily was indignant.

"Her name is Jabberwock, as you very well know," she said.

By the time Tobias was born, I was almost five and the Hall kids were beginning to outnumber the families in the cities where we lived. Sometimes we outnumbered them in children, but we always outnumbered them in cats.

When Susanna was born, Tobias was given Barbara Frietchie, a black-and-white boy kitten with a small white bow tie across his black lips. We were told by the owners that Barbara Frietchie was a girl, which is why we named her Barbara, but the owners happened to be wrong.

"Maybe we should change Barbara's name," my father suggested to Tobias.

"I like the name Barbara Frietchie," Tobias said. "It's a famous name."

The name had actually come from an American history book I had in first grade that had a poem about an old woman in Maryland called Barbara Frietchie. During the Civil War, she had been ordered by the Confederate army to take down the American flag that was hanging from her house. "'Shoot if you must this old gray head, but spare your country's flag,' she said."

By the time we got Barbara Frietchie, my mother had decided that five cats was enough — more than enough when Martha Washington mistook the gas burners on the stove for her kitty litter box.

But that left Susanna kittenless, and so in Edinburgh, Susanna got Parsimonious, who was our only purebred, aristocratic cat, a cross-eyed blue point Siamese who, for complicated reasons I will explain later, was given to us for free by our next-door neighbors.

So, by summer vacation the year we were two, four, six, and eight, when my father was sent to Tokyo as a specialist to train young Japanese pediatric neurosurgeons, we all six marched through the Edinburgh airport with our overnight bags in one hand and our cat boxes in the other, armed for a new city in a new country of the world.

If my father had been in the house in Boston instead of traveling in California, he would have wrapped Rrrr in a towel and put him in a box, and tonight we would bury him in the growing graveyard in the garden. We'd have a prayer, and I would give a small speech about what a good cat Rrrr had been and we'd sing something lonely like, "O, God our help in ages past/ Our hope for years to come," which is what they sang at First Presbyterian when my grandfather died. And Susanna would insist, as she has when this has happened before, that she can see Rrrr flying on silver wings up into the sky.

But my father wasn't there, and I was afraid to go downstairs and even look at Rrrr, who has slept with me every night since I was three years old, under my sheets, lying on my legs, purring so loudly that I could hear him from my pillow. I couldn't imagine being brave enough to pick Rrrr up and wrap him up as my father would have done if he hadn't been traveling. I don't know why. Rrrr was the same cat who was alive when I went to school this morning. But death is like that.

So I sat on my bed watching the clock move slowly as white paste toward five in the afternoon, when my mother and Susanna would be home, hating my school, hating my new house, hating Boston, hating what has happened to our lives since we moved here.

Which is why I'm writing this story today, the day after Rrrr died — because something amazing took place in my bedroom room late last night after our parents were in bed. But before I explain what happened last night, I have to tell you about the terrible year we've had since last August when we moved to this tall, skinny house with a small garden in the back and no front yard, in the middle of Boston, Massachusetts, on a busy street in a neighborhood without any children and very few cats.

September

*

*

Our first day at Eaton Elementary School was beautiful and sunny, and we ate breakfast in the backyard of our new house on Beacon Street. We had big honey donuts and orange juice from the carton and cereal out of paper bowls because nothing had been unpacked since we arrived from Tokyo.

There was nothing unusual about the way we felt the morning of our first day of school at Eaton. We were always arriving at a new house before our packing boxes had arrived from our last home and, of course, we were always starting at a new school, sometimes in the middle of the year. What was different this time was my mother's pep talk.

"We are Americans," our mother told us as if we didn't know that, as if this announcement was news we were hearing for the first time.

"So?" Tobias asked.

"So finally you're going to a school where you will stay until you graduate to the middle school."

"You told us that already," Emily said.

"What I didn't tell you is that the friends you make now — today, this first day and all year long — you won't have to tell good-bye. They will be your friends in elementary school and in middle school and high school and college and even after you get married."

"That's a nightmare," I said.

Which was true. I have no plans to be married ever, and at that particular moment, I had no interest in making any more friends than my brother and sisters and the cats.

The cats were lying around the garden, happily licking their fur with long, scratchy tongues, biting their toenails, stretching belly-up in the sun — all except Jabberwock, who liked to finish the milk in Susanna's cereal bowl.

"I don't think we should let the cats out," I said as my mother brushed the tangles out of Susanna's carrot-colored hair. "They don't know Boston and they might get killed."

"Right," Tobias said. He always agrees with me. I can count on that.

"Cats are extremely smart," Emily said. "Nothing will happen to them."

"They may be smart enough in other places but they're innocent cats," I said. "They aren't really American, so they don't understand what it's like to live here."

"Don't worry, Peter," my mother said. "I'll be careful with the cats."

But I didn't quite trust that my mother would be careful enough. She was too completely happy to be in Boston to worry about trouble.

* * *

We left Tokyo in August. I must have had a sense that our lives in Boston would be miserable from the moment my father announced that we were moving.

"Moving to Boston?" I said, unable to conceal my disappointment. I had in mind South Africa or Korea at the time.

"Your father's been made Director of Pediatric Neurology at Boston Children's Hospital," my mother said. "It's a permanent appointment."

"What does permanent mean?" Susanna asked.

"Don't ask," I said, feeling sick.

"It means forever," Emily said.

"We're moving to Boston forever?" Susanna asked.

I got up from the table then and went into the bedroom we all four shared, taking Rrrr with me for company.

"I feel sick," I said to my father.

Later, after dinner, my father came into the bedroom and sat down at the end of my bed.

"So General, what's the matter?"

He often called me "General."

"Who cares?" I turned away from him.

"I don't understand, Peter," he said. "You have

loved moving more than anyone. So now we're moving again. Why the bad mood?"

"That's the point," I said. "I do love moving, and now we're going someplace to stay."

Later, after everyone was tucked in bed that night and the lights were turned out, my mother leaned over me and whispered goodnight.

"Don't worry," she said. "We're going to love Boston."

I didn't contradict her.

* * *

Except for my father, I was my mother's best friend. Every morning in Tokyo, she walked us to school going all the way up the steps of the building to tell us good-bye before she left for the hospital to help my father with his patients. At the end of the day, she was always waiting at school to walk us home. We'd stop at the market to buy a dinner of rice and fish and vegetables, maybe some sweets. After school, I'd do my homework in the kitchen while my mother cooked. We'd talk about the sick people in the hospital or things at school or the other children in the family, especially Emily, who was having trouble at the American School in Tokyo because her teacher was too strict.

"We'll get a city house with lots of rooms and a garden and you'll play ice hockey or maybe soccer," my mother told me after my father had announced we were moving to Boston. "You could become a wonderful athlete, Peter. With all the traveling we've done, you haven't had a chance for sports," she said.

"Maybe," I said.

"And in Boston, we'll all learn to ice skate," my mother said.

But something felt wrong about Boston from the first day we arrived here, as if the wonderful changes my mother had promised for our lives were not the changes I wanted to happen.

* * *

Eaton Elementary is a half a mile walk from our house, across a few streets without much traffic and then across a large avenue where there is a traffic light and safety guards as well. That first morning, our parents took us to school, and we walked along holding hands, swinging our arms, through groups of children with bookbags and soccer balls and lunchboxes who looked at us with unusual interest. I couldn't blame them. We look interesting. First of all, there are so many of us, and second, we all have red hair. Mine is beigy-red and straight, and I'm tall and skinny with a long, freckled face and a birth-mark in the shape of a strawberry under my chin. Emily's hair is golden-red, striped in the sun, and Susanna's is the color of fresh carrots with curls all over the top, like Tobias's, but he wears his hair very short in a buzz cut so the curls don't show. When we lived in Tokyo, the Japanese people used to stare at us and smile as we walked along the street.

I remember one evening at a restaurant in downtown Tokyo just after we had arrived from Edinburgh. The restaurant was dark and we sat on the floor on low benches at a table with a Japanese family — two children, one my age, one older, and their parents. They were trying not to look at us but they couldn't help themselves. Finally the mother put her hands together as if she were planning to pray and, turning to my parents, said very softly, "I am so sorry to look too much but your children are beautiful red children."

"Thank you," my mother said. "That's very kind of you to say."

It became a joke with us. My father would open the door to the apartment after he came home from work and call out, "Are any of my red children here this evening?"

"Four red children and their cats," we called back.

"Thank goodness. A red child is very scarce in Japan," he said. "They're in great demand and I don't want to lose any of mine."

∗　∗　∗

That first day at Eaton Elementary, we stood in a line just inside the front door where the new students waited to register.

"You'll have to take tests this morning to determine which class you're going to enter," my mother was saying.

"I hate tests," Tobias said.

"They're nothing to worry about," my father said. "A piece of cake."

"Does everyone have to take them?" I asked.

"Not everyone, but you've been in schools all over the world," my mother said. "Your new teachers need to know what you've learned."

"Who cares?" Tobias said, already suspecting the worst.

"I was smart in Tokyo and even smarter in Scotland," Emily said.

"You'll be smart everywhere," my mother said. "Nevertheless, you have to be tested. I had to take a test to get into law school, remember?"

"I remember," I said. "You were in a terrible mood for weeks before the law tests."

"But I passed," she said.

"I know," I said. I wish she had flunked but I didn't tell her that.

The line for new students was long and noisy and what I noticed, especially after going to school in Tokyo, was how difficult it seemed to be for American children to stand still. Three times the principal, Mr. Pesky — who was not much bigger than I am and would have been mistaken for a child except he had a beard — had to ask for silence.

When we finally got to the front of the line, so it was our turn to register and to shake hands with Mr. Pesky (who called me Brian for some reason, although my mother had introduced me as Peter), we were each assigned a "buddy" whose job it was to spend the day with us. The student assigned to me was Buck Dickerson, and the first thing he asked me about was the strawberry mark under my chin. I don't know how he could see it since it doesn't even show unless I lift my head, but I didn't like him, and if he was an example of the other boys at Eaton, I was probably not going to like them any better.

My mother, however, liked Buck Dickerson immediately. She shook his hand and thanked him for his kindness to me — although there hadn't been any evidence of kindness so far — and asked him if he was the tallest boy in the sixth grade.

He shrugged. "I'm pretty tall," he said, "but Ethan's taller than me."

Maybe my mother would prefer to have Buck Dickerson for a son.

"So chicks," my mother said happily as if she couldn't wait to tell us good-bye and race off to her law school classes, "have a wonderful first day of school."

"Knock 'em dead," my father said.

First they kissed Susanna, who trotted off to kindergarten with her new "buddy," and then they kissed Tobias, whose bottom lip was trembling and finally they kissed Emily, who smiled cheerfully. Emily is able to pretend that everything is perfectly fine, even though it isn't.

"Maybe you could start dinner, Em," my mother was saying. "Chop the vegetables I left in the fridge for pasta."

"She could cut herself," I said coolly.

My mother certainly wouldn't have let Emily chop vegetables without grown-up supervision in Tokyo.

"She'll be fine, Peter," my mother said, waving to Emily as she ran up the steps to her classroom.

"I'll be home by seven." She kissed the top of my head.

"Seven?" I asked, stiffening. "That late?"

"It's not so late," my mother said, and then she actually checked her watch, just to make sure I knew that she was in a hurry and didn't have time for my troubles.

When I turned to kiss my father good-bye, as I have done since I was born, he reached out instead and shook my hand.

"See you tonight, son," he said giving me one of those whacks on my shoulder to show what good friends we are.

He had never said good-bye that way before and I wasn't a bit happy about it.

I watched them walk away, my mother tall and slender and blond, her high heels clicking along the floor, my father's blue suit rumpled in the back. And I wished we were back in Tokyo or Scotland or any of the places we had lived before, a tight little family among strangers. Any place except Boston, where the people didn't *seem* to be strangers, but they were.

* * *

Buck was tall and skinny with white-blond hair that he wore sticking up, probably with some greasy stuff to keep it from falling down. He walked with such a long stride, I had to half jog to keep up with him.

"Where'd you go to school before Eaton?" he was asking.

"Tokyo," I said.

"Tokyo?" He said Tokyo with a kind of French accent, as if it were a word he'd never heard before. He said it twice, laughing so hard he fell against the lockers to catch his breath.

"Did you play soccer in Tokyo?" he asked.

I don't play soccer. I've never been anyplace for long enough to join a team, but I made the mistake of telling Buck the truth, and he said that was too bad because ALL of the boys at Eaton played soccer, so I had better learn.

"Or if you turn out to hate soccer, some of the kids do extra work in the library," Buck said in a way that made it quite clear that his friends never got caught in the library unless they had to be there.

I didn't want to learn how to play soccer, but I had a sinking feeling as I followed Buck into the classroom that I wasn't going to have a choice.

According to my mother, I am stubborn and don't like people to tell me what to do. "Anti-authority" is my father's description.

The story about anti-authority that my father likes to tell took place in Washington, D.C., when I was in nursery school. It was the rule at that particular school that children couldn't go to the bathroom by themselves. The teacher, whose name was Sallie Case and who was pretty, would take the child into the bathroom and watch him pee. I don't have any idea why this school had such a peculiar rule but they did. When I asked to be excused to go to the bathroom, Ms. Case said that would be fine and took my hand, walking down the corridor to the bathroom.

"Alone," I said to her once we were inside the door of the boys' room.

"Alone?" she asked.

"I mean I won't go if you're there."

"This is a school rule, Peter. When you're in kindergarten, you can go by yourself." She was probably looking in the mirror fixing her hair, which was long and blond, but I don't remember. I do remember that I had to pee so bad it was filling my eyes with tears.

"My mother won't allow anyone to come to the bathroom with me," I said.

"Your mother is in charge at home and we are in charge at school," Sallie Case said. She may have been pretty but as it turned out, she wasn't very smart. By the time my mother came with Emily and Tobias to pick me up for lunch, I was still in the bathroom arguing with Sallie Case, and there was quite a large circle of pee on my corduroys.

"I'm not going to do stupid things simply because people tell me to, even if they're teachers," I told my father later that evening.

And now, that included soccer.

Buck showed me my desk, my locker, the book-case where our reading and social studies books were kept, and the boys' bathroom. He introduced me to a few boys gathered around the lockers out-side the classroom — a "This is Peter, these are the guys" kind of introduction — and then he went off with his friends to play soccer and left me with the girls.

"See you after the bell rings," he called as he headed down the steps to the playground. "We play soccer every morning before school."

* * *

The test my mother had mentioned was simple, and I took it in the back of the classroom while the other sixth-graders were discussing their unit on South Africa. At recess, the homeroom teacher, Mr. Levine, told me my test was "A-okay" and to go on out to play soccer with the boys.

At the playground, I stood on the edge of the blacktop with the girls. Not actually with them, but close enough to overhear what they were talking about and to come to the conclusion that I had better learn to play soccer soon.

They were talking about their periods and who had gotten it and who hadn't, and their breasts and who had a bra and who didn't.

"I think Miranda got a bra this summer — maybe it's a junior bra but I *know* she doesn't have her period," I overheard one girl saying.

"Well I got my period," another girl said. "And it was *awful*."

"Weird," the first girl said.

I glanced over just to see what these girls looked like and one of them, larger than I was with curly hair twice the size of her head, was looking straight at me.

"You know who I hate?" she was saying.

"No," another girl said.

"Three people. Mary Gates for one."

"So do I," the other girl said.

"Brenda Tappan and Missy *Whatshername*."

"I like Missy okay. She has had her period since I don't know, maybe the middle of fifth grade."

I moved away when the conversation turned to the boys they liked in the sixth grade. It wasn't the kind of talk I'd ever heard in fifth grade in Tokyo or in Rome or Scotland or any place I'd ever lived, for that matter. And I didn't want to hear it now.

I decided to lean against the brick school building, my hands in my pockets, looking across the playground as if I had something important on my mind, and hoping if anyone happened to be watching me, that I seemed to be happy standing alone.

I suppose I was shocked. In the schools where I'd been all over the world, we usually wore uniforms, spoke in full sentences especially in class and didn't use swear words. I had never even imagined girls talking the way I had just overheard the girls at Eaton Elementary speak, although of course I was never at a girl's sleepover or movie party. It occurred to me that Emily could turn out to be just like these girls if we stayed in Boston any longer. Susanna too. Both of them were good at making friends, especially Emily. Much better than me. It's not that I'm shy, although I tend to be quiet until I know people better. But I am hesitant in unfamiliar situations. I don't like to try anything unless I'm sure I can do it, especially in athletics, although I'm told I'm a good athlete. It takes a while for people, especially kids, to get to know me, which is why in all the years we lived in different places, I never made a good friend — friends of course — but not a best friend. I'm not the kind of guy who walks into a new school and by the second day is right in the thick of things as if he's been there for years. But Emily is.

When the first bell for the end of recess rang, I was looking for Emily over in the corner of the playground by the jungle gym where the fourth grade was sent to play during recess. I could see her red hair sparkling yellow in the sunlight, her new green jumper and her high-top sneakers. And then I walked across the asphalt to say hello.

That was a mistake. Emily had a funny expression on her face when she saw me coming, a "where have I ever seen you before?" kind of look. I waved to her and called out "Hi, Em-slem" just so everyone would know that my relationship to her was personal. But she turned her back, flung her arm around the shoulder of a small blond-haired girl in jeans. Another giggly girl, taller than Emily, whispered in her ear.

Emily is not unkind by nature, but sometimes she acts that way because she's self-conscious. She worries about things like whether her friends like her or not, or whether her hair is too short or too long or if she has on the wrong clothes. The right clothes particularly worry Emily. We were almost late for school this morning while she tried on one outfit after another before she decided on the new green jumper. Even then, on the way to school, she asked my mother, "What if no one wears jumpers in Boston?"

"We wouldn't have found jumpers in a Boston store if no one is wearing them, Emily," my mother said.

"I liked it better when we had uniforms," Emily said. "Then I didn't have anything to decide."

Normally, I'm not bothered by Emily, but at that moment on the playground, feeling my world slip out from under me, I was furious, and had a conversation with my mother in my head.

"Since we moved to Boston, Emily is turning into a snob," is how I planned to begin the complaint. And then I was going to tell her about the conversations I overheard among the sixth-grade girls.

When the bell rang for the end of recess, I walked by the second-grade classrooms looking in, checking for Tobias to see how his test went. I didn't see Tobias, but Susanna came out of the girls' room, holding the hand of a little girl about her size.

"That's Peter," she told her new friend, too busy to talk to me. "He's my brother."

"Hi," I said and stopped, but Susanna went on, looking back at me over her shoulder.

"See you later, alligator," I called.

"See you later, alligator?" she giggled. "I'm not an alligator. I'm a girl."

* * *

I have always been the one in charge. In Tokyo and Rome and Edinburgh, ever since I've been old enough, my parents have left the other children with me. Sometimes I walked them to school and to dance classes and to sports. I've even gone to films with them if my parents were busy at the hospital. I'm almost, I guess you could say, like a father to them. And to the cats as well. We all take care of our own cats, but sometimes Susanna or Tobias forgets — even Emily forgets — and so I end up changing the kitty litter on someone else's turn, or filling the bowls with Meow Mix.

But my main job has been my brother and sisters, particularly since we kept moving to new cities and new schools whose customs were unfamiliar to us. My parents count on me. Even teachers have understood my responsibilities and have depended on me as well.

Once, when we were living in Rome, Susanna disappeared. My mother had taken her to nursery school, but by milk and crackers time, the nursery school teacher noticed that Susanna was missing.

"Peter," the teacher screamed, flying into my classroom. "I need you immediately. I spoke sharply to Susanna, and now she has disappeared."

Generally, I'm good in emergencies. I don't get too excited and I never cry.

I followed the nursery school teacher back to Susanna's classroom and in a couple of minutes, I had found my sister in the broom closet at the back of the room, sitting in a bucket full of mops.

"I don't know what I would have done without Peter," the teacher told my mother that afternoon when she came to pick us up.

"We don't know what we'd do without him either," my mother said.

Until this year, I felt important in my family, indispensable.

✳ ✳ ✳

After recess, I walked down the corridor behind Buck and his soccer playing friends, up the steps into the crowded lunchroom, got a plate of cardboard with ketchup (called lasagna) and sat down next to some girls from my class, who were discussing their sex education class.

I could tell I wasn't going to be happy at this school.

I finished my lunch quickly, dumped my trash, put my tray on the conveyor belt, and was just walking out the door to go to homeroom when the second grade arrived for lunch. Tobias was at the end of the line.

"Guess what?" he said, pulling me aside and whispering in my ear.

"What? " I asked.

"I have a learning problem," he said.

I could tell he was about to cry.

"How do you know?" I asked. "You've never had a learning problem before."

"I took that test we had to take to see how smart we are," Tobias said.

"Right," I said. "I did too."

"And I overheard my teacher say to the assistant that I have a learning problem," Tobias said.

"Well, they're wrong," I said.

Tobias shrugged.

"I liked it better in Tokyo," he said.

"Same here," I said, and walked down the corridor, passing the large poster along the walls: WELCOME TO EATON ELEMENTARY SCHOOL.

October

Our house in Boston is one of those very skinny houses attached to other houses on both sides so there are only windows on the front and back. In the case of our house, these windows are large, and the house itself is very tall. Four stories. I am on the top floor with my own bedroom and bath, and my father's study is across the tiny hall. The large windows are called sash windows, which means they have panes and slide up and down. All of the windows except the ones in my father's study have screens. According to my mother, my parents didn't notice there weren't any screens in my father's study until October seventh.

October was hot this year, so mostly we kept the windows in the house open.

The night of October seventh, the week of soccer tryouts for the sixth grade, I heard my parents in their bedroom, which is on the third floor, talking (I thought) about me. So I got out of bed, crept barefoot to the top of the stairs, got down on my stomach, and leaned over the first four steps to listen to what they were saying. I could hear them clearly, and just as I suspected, they were talking about me.

"Peter's changed," my mother was saying. "I don't think he's adjusting to Eaton very well."

I guessed that my father was sitting up in bed, reading *Science Magazine,* not much interested in my adjustment. My father loves us very much, but he doesn't like to talk about the personal details in our lives unless they have to do with school or illness.

So my mother, whose name is Gail, said in an exasperated voice, "Jonathan," (my father's name) "are you listening to me?"

"Of course I'm listening. I'm a great listener," my father said. "Peter's a trouper. He'll be fine."

"He's not fine," my mother said. "All the other children have made friends, even Tobias has Ricky Seamore and Gregory Something-or-other to go to the movies with. And Emily and Susanna have hundreds of birthday party invitations and sleepovers. But Peter does nothing except hang around the house and play with the cats."

Which is true, of course. Emily and I used to be the ones who spent our time playing with the cats. We were required to be with them. We were the cats' parents. In this game we had played almost every day, I had a job as an airline pilot flying big-body jets and Emily was a film star. When we got home from school Emily would put on one of my mother's gowns and I would wear my father's shoes and old glasses (out of which I could hardly see) and we would have dinner with the cats. This was usually in my bedroom with the door shut so the cats, who were not exactly happy to be with us, couldn't get out. We'd set a table with knives and forks and plates on which we would put cat food, and then we'd sit down at either end of the table to discuss the day.

"Glimmer was a nightmare today," Emily would say. "First off, she peed on our bed."

"Jeez, Glimmer," I'd say to my mother's cat, who was eating her dry food from one of the dishes we usually use for our own dinner. "I think you're developing personality problems."

"When we get back to the States, we'll get a psychiatrist," Emily would say.

"How did your math test go today, Rrrr?" I'd ask Rrrr, who prowled along the closed door to the bedroom waiting for an escape and refused to eat dinner at the table, preferring his own dish on the kitchen floor.

"He flunked the math test," Emily said. "The teacher called to tell me Rrrr is bored in third grade."

"Of course he's bored," I'd say, understanding completely Rrrr's predicament in math. "And how was your day, darling?" I'd imitate my father's first question to my mother when he comes home from the hospital at night.

"Drop the darling." Emily would flash me a look. "My day was wonderful. I have a new part

in a film as a beautiful singer who dies tragi-
cally of cancer or maybe a car accident. I can't remember."

"You're absolutely sure she's beautiful?" I'd ask.

"Of course I'm sure," Emily would reply.

We could play that game for a long time but
usually Tobias or Susanna — or both — would
arrive and we'd have to stop because they always
refused to play the roles of our children or the cats.
So there was nothing for them to do.

* * *

I slid on my belly down a couple more steps so I
wouldn't miss anything my parents were saying.
Rrrr had followed me, purring in my ear, swiping
his tail across my face.

"Shh," I said to Rrrr, because it was difficult to
hear with the sound of purring, but by then my
father had gotten out of bed, and was calling to my
mother, probably from the other side of the bedroom, where he keeps the medical books that he
likes to read before he goes to sleep. I could hear

everything, and so could Susanna, who sleeps on the same floor of the house.

"What about soccer?" he asked. "Didn't I hear you say they're having tryouts this week?"

"I don't know, Jonathan. Peter's not a very good soccer player since he hasn't had the chance to play, so I'm afraid he may not be asked to join the team," my mother said. "And then what?"

"It won't be the end of the world," my father said. "He'll figure out something else. Peter's resilient."

*　*　*

I don't know what resilient means, but I doubt very much that I have it. Especially now, feeling weak with homesickness every day, which is surprising. Here I am at home with my family and my cats so you probably would ask, "Homesick for what?" And I would answer, "Homesick for the way we used to live before we came to Boston."

Ever since I was nine, which made Emily seven, Tobias five, and Susanna three, we've had a pact. We call it the "First Pact." The name was actually given to us by my father when he overheard us talking in the living room in Scotland.

"I think we should make a pact about friends," I was saying. "We can have friends of course but we are always each other's *first* friends."

"Best friends," Emily said.

"First friends," I said. "Which means we come first before any of our other friends."

"A First Pact," my father said.

"Exactly," I agreed.

"So if I have a friend ask me over and you want to play, you come first," Emily said.

"That's right," I said.

It was easy to keep the promises of the "First Pact" when we lived all over the world. By the time any of us had even made a friend, we were packing up to move to a new country.

In Boston, however, the "First Pact" has been a failure.

* * *

Initially, I wasn't going to try out for soccer, but my father said, "Go for it," and my mother said, "You'll make some new friends if you do try out." Which was true, and so I did try.

I am not good.

"How bad are you?" Buck asked me on the first day of tryouts.

"Pretty bad," I said.

We were sitting on the bench waiting for our turn to try out and I was nervous, although I kept telling myself that it didn't make a bit of difference. Why should it? If I didn't make the team, there was always the possibility of going to school someplace else, maybe Paris.

When my name was called, I ran out to the field, feeling awkward, duck-footed. As I've said, I'm a good athlete but changing schools every year and living all over the world hasn't allowed for me to develop any skills. For example, I couldn't really dribble the ball. So there I was in the middle of the field at tryouts, playing center forward, and the ball came to me, kicked pretty hard by Gunner, who is a boy in my class, and then I was dribbling the ball down the field and fell over it. Simply tripped and fell flat on my chest, and while I was lying there trying to catch my breath, since I hit the ground hard enough to knock the air out of me, I could hear the rest of the team laughing. Or I thought I could hear them.

"I told you I wasn't very good." I was walking back to the locker room with Gunner and Buck and Buck's best friend, Jimbo.

"Don't worry about it," Buck said.

"I'm bad too," Jimbo said. "I mean, last year I only just made the team."

"I kicked it pretty hard," Gunner said. "It might've knocked you off balance."

I shrugged.

"Gunner's number one on the team," Buck said.

"Number two," Gunner corrected. "Andy Saile is number one."

"Anyhow, you'll get another chance tomorrow," Buck said. "We all get two tries and then the coach announces the team on Friday."

"And if you don't make it, you'll get another chance next year," Gunner said.

Gunner was probably trying to be nice, but I put his name as number seventeen on the list I kept in my brain of the kids I didn't like since I had arrived at Eaton Elementary.

✳   ✳   ✳

The second tryout was today and it was a disaster. Just after the whistle, in my first play of the afternoon, I was dribbling down the field, no one around me, and I had a clear shot at the goal, close in, the goalie standing right in the middle of the goal. I could have shot the ball on either side of him, but instead, I gave the ball a huge kick and *bamm-o*, over the net and out.

Walking away from tryouts today, Buck told me that maybe I'd get better in soccer if I practiced.

"Don't count on making the team," he said.

"Not a chance I'll make it," I said.

"But some of the guys who don't make the team play with the fifth-graders so they can improve their skills."

"I probably won't have time for that," I said as if I was *so* interested in playing soccer that I'd be willing to play with the fifth-graders.

* * *

I was just about to get up from the steps and go into my parents' room to tell them why I hated soccer and wasn't going to make the team, when a loud screech came from the bedroom across from my parents, and Susanna burst into the hall, screaming that Parsimonious had disappeared.

Parsimonious was my favorite cat, next to Rrrr. She had shiny white fur with a whisper of gray, crossed blue eyes, and very large, funny ears peaked like a teepee. But, as I told you earlier, we got her for free, even though she should have been expensive since she's a purebred. And she was free because she was stupid. Even her owners knew that when she was a kitten. She had a kind of cockeyed way of walking, rocking back and forth on her tiny paws, a way of holding her head tilted as if it might fall off, and a habit of falling flat on her face.

As you probably know, cats have amazing balance. They can walk on ledges without falling and jump from great heights, landing on all four feet.

But not Parsimonious. Put Parsimonious on the kitchen counter and *kerplop* — off she went, squashed onto the linoleum. She jumped up on things perfectly well, but she never learned how to get down. Since we've had her — and she's the youngest of our cats, only three years old — she's broken a leg once and a foot once and bloodied her face falling off the kitchen counter.

That's really what I loved best about Parsimonious. She needed help.

At night she slept with Susanna. All of our cats sleep with us — Glimmer at my mother's feet, Martha Washington at my father's feet, Jabberwock under the covers with Emily, Barbara Frietchie on Tobias's pillow, Rrrr under my arm, and Parsimonious curled around Susanna's head. That's where she had been on the night of October seventh, when my mother finished reading to Susanna and turned out her bedside light.

* * *

Susanna was standing in the middle of the hall crying at the top of her voice, waking Tobias and Emily who sleep on the second floor and they ran upstairs to see what was the matter.

"I'm sure Parsimonious is somewhere in the house," my mother said, rushing out of her bedroom in her robe. "Maybe getting something to eat as usual."

We all ran downstairs, through the hall, into the kitchen, and turned on the light. There was cat food in the ceramic bowl beside the back door. But Parsimonious wasn't there.

"I'll check the living room," Tobias said. "Sometimes she sleeps on the couch."

My mother had turned on the light in the dining room.

"Check upstairs, Peter," my mother said to me.

"Maybe she's under Susanna's bed, " Emily said.

"She's not," I said. "I looked already."

"She never goes under my bed," Susanna said. "She's afraid of the dark."

Tobias and Emily had checked their rooms and the bathroom and my mother checked the basement, even though the door down to the basement was kept shut. I ran up the three flights of stairs to my bedroom where Rrrr was lying at the foot of my bed with a funny expression on his face that I had never seen before.

The light was on in my father's study. I walked across the corridor from my room and there was my father at the open window, his back to me, leaning out over the garden, thirty feet down.

He must not have heard me come in. He closed the window behind his desk, and turned around with a sudden, startled look on his face when he saw me.

"Parsimonious?" I asked, knowing of course what he had seen when he leaned out over the garden.

He nodded.

Later, we sat around the kitchen table and my mother let us have cookies and hot chocolate, even though it was almost midnight.

"I'm so sorry," my mother kept saying. "I'm so sorry, Susanna."

It looked to me as if my father was crying, but I didn't bring it up.

"Poor, poor Parsimonious," Susanna had her head down on the kitchen table. "It's my fault for letting her go upstairs to Daddy's study."

"Of course it isn't your fault," my father said. "I should have made sure that all of the windows had screens."

"We didn't think enough about the cats," Susanna said. "I even forgot to tell Parsimonious to watch out in Boston."

"Peter was right," Emily said. "We have to be particularly careful with the cats in Boston because this house is more dangerous than other houses we've lived in."

"It's not dangerous," my mother said, defending our new lives. "This could have happened any place. It's our fault, not the fault of Boston or of this house."

I didn't tend to agree with my mother as much as I used to. Boston might not have deliberately set out to make life difficult for us or for our cats, but it was certainly true that Parsimonious was the same screwy-minded cat without much common sense when we had lived in Tokyo and Rome and Edinburgh, and nothing had happened to her there.

"This house is four stories high and on a busy street," Tobias said.

"We just have to be more cautious with the cats until they adjust," my mother said quietly.

"I know." Susanna climbed on Emily's lap and buried her face.

"A lot more careful," I said.

I didn't like the fact that my mother was defending the stupid house when we had just had a family tragedy.

"You seem to care more about houses than living creatures," I said to her in front of everybody.

I love my mother and think she's remarkable and wonderful, but I was beginning to wonder whether she was changing into someone else who went to law school in business suits, interested only in books and briefs and arguments from somebody else's life.

"I don't need to defend myself, Peter," my mother said coolly. "You know how I feel about the cats."

I wasn't going to let the subject go.

"I thought I knew," I said.

"That's enough," my father interrupted and he meant it. "We've had a sad night and it's not going to end up in a fight."

Later I asked him why we had fought after Parsimonious was killed, since normally we don't fight very often.

"When something bad happens, people who love each other sometimes fight," he said. "It makes them feel better to blame someone."

"You mean like me with Mom?" I asked.

"Like that," he said. "But the real fault with Parsimonious was mine for leaving the window open without a screen."

That night we slept in our parents' bed, all of us and our cats, squeezed in, side by side. I lay on my back, between Tobias and my father, my arms wrapped around Rrrr, my eyes wide open, looking at the ceiling, at the lights from the cars as they passed the busy street in front of our house, at the long, gray shadows moving across the wall.

November

*

The day after Parsimonious died, Susanna sat in my mother's lap on the couch in the living room and cried. For two days, she wouldn't go to school, and refused to go on play-dates or to the zoo with her new best friend Suki Smith or to a sleepover at Bess's house. But by Monday she was fine.

By the end of a week Susanna had completely forgotten about Parsimonious. I don't know how she did it.

I don't forget anything. Every place we've lived sits in a corner of my mind as if my memory is a building of furnished apartments from all over the world and our family has lived in every one of them with our cats. I remember things particularly if I think about the cats.

I was tiny but I remember when Rrrr was brought home as a kitten. I slept with my parents in Accra on a mattress on the floor beside their bed. My mattress was covered with netting to protect me from mosquitoes because the mosquitoes in Africa often carry malaria. Rrrr had very long sharp claws and the netting drove him wild. He'd paw at it and his claws would get caught, which made him yowl, and when I'd finally gotten him unstuck, he'd paw at the netting again.

"Please go to sleep, Peter," my mother would say when the commotion began.

"Rrrr's stuck again," I'd say.

"Maybe it would be better if he didn't sleep with you."

"He has to," I'd say quietly pulling Rrrr's paws free of the string.

∗ ∗ ∗

I remember the living room of our apartment in Prague, which was where we were living when

Emily got Jabberwock. Even now, we don't know whether Jabberwock is brain-damaged or not — although we always say she is. In the first place, most cats eat only when they're hungry. If you put a huge bowl of food out for them, they will finish it little by little, but not all at once. That's not true of Jabberwock. If we put two weeks of food in her bowl, she'll eat it all in one sitting and then she'll explode. My father says she is missing an apostat, which is the gauge in her brain that should tell her when she's full. And secondly, she smiles out of the corner of her mouth — a crooked smile that makes her look demented. And maybe she is.

Our living room in Prague looked like one of those very old-fashioned oil paintings of the interior of houses. It was dark with heavy furniture and scratchy slipcovers in maroons and dark greens. There were chandeliers. We loved it because it was like a castle.

One afternoon before we knew about Jabberwock's apostat, I put out enough food for all of the cats, and Jabberwock, who was still a kitten, ate every bit of it and then fell over with a belly the size of a tennis ball and finally threw up on the Oriental carpet.

Other people like Barbara Frietchie the best of all our cats because of the way he looks in his black tuxedo and white bow tie. He is also more polite than the rest of our cats. He doesn't jump up on the laps of strangers or wind his sleek black body through their legs as cats like to do, and he doesn't meow. Ever. He sits on his haunches in a shaft of sunlight with his feet straight in front of him, his head forward, a serious-looking statue of a cat who is amusing to look at but doesn't require a relationship with human beings for his personal happiness.

My sweetest memory of Parsimonious is in Japan in the evenings when the moon lit our bedroom with enough filtered silver light to outline her soft white body, wrapped around Susanna's bright red head like a cap.

"I think about Parsimonious every day," I told my mother one morning before school while she was rushing around getting breakfast ready.

Susanna wasn't in the kitchen that morning. She had spent the night at Suki Smith's.

"So do I, darling," she said in that offhand way she has developed when she's thinking about something else.

"So something must be the matter with Susanna since she never thinks about Parsimonious anymore," I said loading my oatmeal with brown sugar. "Maybe she's insensitive."

"She's not insensitive," my mother said sitting down beside me at the table with her coffee. "She's young and sometimes young children recover from sadness more easily."

"I'd be more worried if Susanna was moping around the house," my father said from behind the newspaper, which is where he spends breakfast.

So I dropped the subject of Susanna until Tobias and Emily and I were walking to school.

"I like Susanna better than I used to because finally she's getting grownup," Tobias said. "She doesn't come crying to me every five minutes like she used to do."

"I think you should give Susanna a break and think about yourself," Emily said, busy waving to just about everybody we passed on the way to school.

"Think about myself? What does that mean?" I asked.

"You're in a bad mood every single day," Emily said, flying up the front steps at Eaton Elementary to catch up with her friends.

I suppose that Emily was right. I *was* in a terrible mood. I used to think of Susanna as an angel with her top knot of red curls and dimples and sunshine smile. We spent hours together, playing made-up stories that were a little immature for me, but I played because Susanna thought I was perfect. The best brother in the world.

Now that she's changed since we moved to Boston, I couldn't stop thinking about her.

"Susanna's perfectly normal," my mother said to me when I suggested that something was seriously wrong with her. "Don't fret. She's got a lot of friends."

"Too many," I said. "It isn't normal to have fourteen best friends."

"But she's very happy," my mother said. "You're the one who isn't happy here, darling."

When I complained to Emily, she said that Susanna was growing up.

"I like her better than ever," Emily told me, echoing Tobias. "She's getting to be more like a girl than a baby."

"Of course you do," I said. "She spends all her time trying to turn into you. She imitates the whispery way you talk and she wants to wear your clothes and your shoes and grow her hair long like yours and probably have it dyed from carrot to golden-red."

Emily shrugged.

"That's what little sisters are like."

"Tobias doesn't feel that way about me."

"Tobias has a learning problem."

"He didn't feel that way about me before he had a learning problem."

"I think you're jealous because Susanna used to like you better than anyone and now she has a lot of friends."

I didn't reply to Emily, suddenly feeling cold all over, the way you do when you hear the truth and it's not what you want to hear.

"It isn't jealousy," I said finally, but I wasn't exactly sure what I was feeling. Not good. I was sure about that.

* * *

I didn't make the soccer team. I wasn't the only one.
There were about ten other boys in the sixth grade
who didn't make it, but they were mostly the kind
who didn't care about soccer, boys like my father
probably used to be, who like science or board
games or reading books in the library or examining
plants in the botanical garden down the street from
where we lived.

So by Thanksgiving I hadn't made any friends.
I'd only been invited to two birthday parties and
everyone in the class went to those. I was never
asked to a sleepover, although Buck and his best
friend, Jimbo, asked me to go to the drugstore to
read comic books with them, and we sat around the
magazine section a couple of times eating candy
bars. I actually was having a good time until Buck
brought up the subject of Emily.

"Your sister Emily spent the night on Saturday,"
Buck said.

"I know," I said.

"She says you hate Eaton."

"I don't hate Eaton," I said, furiously thinking of what I would say to Emily the next time I saw her. "We used to have a different kind of life than we have now, living all over the world, moving every year or so and now we've come to Boston to stay."

"You don't like Boston?" Jimbo asked in a way that I knew I better like Boston or we weren't going to be friends.

"I like it okay," I said.

When I got home, Emily was in the kitchen chopping vegetables for dinner. Barbara Frietchie was lying on the table licking the water off the broccoli.

"Thanks a lot for telling Buck that I don't like Eaton or Boston," I said. "That was very helpful to my popularity in the sixth grade."

"You don't like Eaton and they know it," Emily said. "Buck brought it up. I didn't."

"You could have lied."

"Buck asked me *why* you didn't like Eaton. Not *if* you did."

"I used to be able to count on you Emily," I said,

picking up Rrrr and heading upstairs to my bed-room. "You used to be not only my sister but my loyal friend."

"I still am, if you'd only notice," Emily said, pil-ing the raw vegetables in a mixing bowl and putting it in the fridge.

✳ ✳ ✳

My parents were concerned. Concerned is my mother's word and she used it about me all the time during the fall. But even my father was concerned, which is rare since he is interested in the brains of children as they appear under a microscope. I never think of him worrying about something as simple as whether or not I have friends.

"I haven't met anyone I like," I said to him on Thanksgiving afternoon while the other children were taking a walk with my grandmother from Florida.

"You don't have to like them," my father said.

We were peeling potatoes and slicing apples for pie and chopping onions on the cutting board.

"You just have to be interested in them," he continued. "You won't know whether you *like* them until you're interested in them."

I had thought about my predicament. Of course, there were boys in my class I could like, even some girls. And I *could* work harder to make friends and invite people over and hang out after school and play pick-up soccer on the field behind the elementary school. But I didn't.

"I think you may be depressed, Peter," my mother said.

"I am depressed because Parsimonious was killed and nobody in the family seems to care a bit about it," I said. "I'm very depressed about that."

"I don't think it's entirely about Parsimonious," my mother said.

"No. It's also about Eaton, which I hate, and Boston and the way the rest of the family is so happy here it makes me sick."

"It's about change," my mother said, speaking sweetly as if it really mattered to her that I was unhappy. As if something besides law school was important.

"I don't like change if that's what you're wondering," I said, and out of nowhere, sitting right there peeling potatoes, while my father sat on the stool next to me and chopped onions, I had a feeling of sudden and overpowering anger.

"I *hate* change," I said furiously, my face hot, my eyes wet.

Sometimes feelings come over me like weather, tornados blowing over the horizon, a black cloud swirling out of control in my direction.

I had never thought about change before because in the past we were always moving to another place. But my mother was right. Moving to Boston was a *real* change because this time we were staying in one place, one house, one school.

"I really hate it and everything that's happened since we moved here."

"Then *you* have to be the one to change, darling," my mother said, in that certain knowing way she has that I *sometimes* like if she's talking to one of the other children, but I *never* like if she's talking to me. "You can't allow the changes that happen outside you determine the way your life is."

"Right. You're one hundred percent right," I said, putting down a half-peeled potato, picking up Rrrr who was sleeping under the kitchen table hoping for droppings of food. "Thanks a lot for your advice."

I threw Rrrr over my shoulder.

"Count me out for Thanksgiving dinner," I called taking the stairs two at a time, up three flights, to my room where I went in, shut the door, and turned out the light.

Wherever we have lived, we have always had Thanksgiving dinner. Even last year in Tokyo, my mother decided the chickens looked yellow and sickly, so she got fish instead. We stuffed the fish with bread crumbs and onions, pretending it was a turkey, and had rice decorated with tiny paper American flags that my father got at the American embassy.

✳ ✳ ✳

We always sing "Over the river and through the woods to Grandmother's house we go," which is a funny song for us to sing since one of my grand-mothers lives in a high rise in New Jersey and the other lives in a high rise in Florida, and there are no woods or river to go through to see them. But we have pretended a lot of things living all over the world.

I turned on my stomach, put Rrrr over my head like a pillow so I couldn't hear the noises of my family from the first floor and tried to sleep.

I don't like kids who act like I'm acting now. They drive me crazy, but I can't seem to help it. Sometimes I listen to myself whining away like a baby, and it makes me sick and I wonder how any-one in the world would even want to have me as a friend or to sleep over at his house or go to his birthday party.

Sometimes, I simply feel so terrible, I want to sleep through the morning and the afternoon into the dark. Which is what happened to me Thanksgiving afternoon.

When I woke up, Susanna was on my pillow, looking at me with her bright, blue eyes, her funny little smile turned up like a comma, her red top knot.

"Hi," she said.

I must have given her a mean look — I have a few mean looks I use when I need to — because she scrunched up her face as if she were going to cry.

"How come you're always mad at me?" she asked.

"I'm not," I said.

"Yes, you are," she said. "You've been mad ever since Parsimonious died."

I turned over, sat up and dumped Rrrr on the floor.

"You think I don't care that Parsimonious died," Susanna said. "That's what Mommy told me."

"Maybe," I folded my arms across my chest. "Maybe I do."

"Well, you're wrong. When it gets dark at night and I'm in my bed where Parsimonious used to sleep and the stars come out, I'm very sad," Susanna said. "But in the day, I have to do things and play with my friends and do my work. Or else."

"Or else what?" I asked.

Susanna shrugged. "Or else something worse."

She hopped down off the bed.

"I'm supposed to tell you it's Thanksgiving dinner," she said.

"I'm not hungry," I said.

"That's what Daddy said you would say but you have to come," Susanna said picking up Rrrr, throwing him over her small shoulder, and heading downstairs. "It's Thanksgiving, dumbbell, and we all have to be there or else."

"Or else what?" I asked, but I'd already made up my mind.

"Or else worse," she said.

And I couldn't help smiling.

After she left, I got out of bed, went into the bathroom, splashed water on my face, and feeling better for the cold water and Susanna's visit, I flew down the three floors of stairs to the dining room where my family was already seated around the table waiting for my arrival.

December

Christmas is my favorite holiday and not because of the presents. In fact, during the years we lived in other countries, we didn't get presents. We'd fill my father's old socks with candy and small, junky toys and hang them on the fireplace — if we had one — or by the front door, if we didn't.

What we did do was spend the night before Christmas in the same bed, all four of us telling ghost stories, trying to make up the scariest story, or bloodiest or creepiest or worst story. We'd scream and shriek and on Christmas Eve my parents never told us to be quiet and go to sleep. They kissed us goodnight and told us "Merry Christmas."

On Christmas morning, we'd talk about our family.

I can't explain it exactly, but there we'd all be in an apartment that belonged to someone else, sitting on someone else's furniture, with someone else's pictures on the walls, and their pots and pans and dishes, which is how we lived when we moved from country to country, in borrowed houses. We'd sit around our pretend Christmas tree made by my mother of branches and ribbons and popcorn and cookies, eating cake and drinking hot tea with honey and singing Christmas carols before we opened the boxes containing our cats, which we had just wrapped.

"I love it here," I'd say wherever we happened to be, Tokyo or Edinburgh or Rome.

"Me too," Tobias would say.

"Especially me," Susanna added.

"I love it with the family," Emily said. "It doesn't matter where we live as long as we're all together."

"That's because we have the best family on earth," Susanna said.

"On earth and in the whole world," Tobias added.

"Which is the same thing," I said.

"Well," my father would say in his balanced, scientific way, uncomfortable with exaggerated statements like the ones we liked to make. "There are many nice families and we are lucky to have one of them."

And then we'd unwrap our cats.

We did this every year, although Tobias always worried that one of the cats would suffocate in spite of the holes we poked in the boxes for air and Susanna didn't exactly understand why it was necessary to wrap the cats as presents since they lived with us every day of the year.

I'd open my box and Rrrr would step out looking a little forlorn after his morning in a box. I'd tie a red ribbon around his neck, kiss him on the lips, and wish him Merry Christmas.

"Look what I got," Emily would say, lifting a befuddled Jabberwock out of the box, decorating her for the holiday. "A yellow cat."

"You knew it was a cat," Susanna said, confused. "You put her in the box and wrapped her up."

"I'm going to name her Jabberwock," Emily said. "Jabberwock T. Hall."

"Her name is already Jabberwock," Susanna said, opening her package with Parsimonious inside, who climbed out of the box and licked herself from top to bottom.

"It's only Parsimonious," Susanna said sadly.

"Did you think she would change into an actual present?" Tobias asked.

"I think this is a dumb game," Susanna said. "I'd like Christmas with real presents, not the cats we already have."

This Christmas was going to be entirely different.

One Monday in December, I came home to find a large fir tree on the porch leaning against the railing and a wreath with red velvet ribbons on the front door.

"Isn't it too early for Christmas?" I asked when I went into the living room to find my mother unpacking shopping bags of ornaments and tiny lights.

"We've never had a *real* Christmas before,

darling," she said. "This year we're going to have everything, lights and wreaths and ornaments and stockings and Christmas music playing on the tape deck."

"That's too bad," I said wandering into the kitchen, dropping my bookbag, slipping into a kitchen chair.

"What's too bad?" she asked.

"I thought we had always had a *real* Christmas," I said.

I watched her take a tray of cookies shaped like stars out of the oven and sprinkle the tops with red-and-green glitter.

"Want one?" she asked, taking a hot cookie herself.

"No thanks," I said, leaning my chin in my hands.

I could tell I was hurting her feelings but I couldn't help it.

"I'm not actually hungry," I said.

She filled a bowl with nuts and candy canes, opened a box she had bought and took out a large reindeer candlestick with a place for the candle in a hole on his back. She picked up a shopping bag full of something large and asked me if I could keep a secret.

I nodded.

She held up a pair of white ice skates.

"For Emily," she said.

"She doesn't know how to ice skate," I said.

"But she will," my mother said. "We're all going to learn to ice skate this winter."

"It doesn't look like a lot of fun to me," I said. "Especially the falling down part."

"Well, you don't have to come with us," she said, her voice edgy with irritation. "You can sit at home in your room and complain to Rrrr about your terrible life."

I unpacked my books, making a stack of them on the kitchen table where we did our homework, looked in the fridge for a snack and took out a bottle of apple juice. My mother was right about me but I didn't plan to let her know that.

"So," I said casually, as if it didn't matter whatsoever. "We're having real presents this year."

"We are," she said forgetting how cross she had

been at me just a minute ago. "You kids have missed something by having those tiny little Christmases all over the world, while your Daddy and I had wonderful Christmases when we were growing up, with dinners and parties and presents and stockings."

"I liked the little tiny Christmases," I said, picking Rrrr up from under the table where he was sleeping, his tiger paw covering his eyes. I headed for the stairs.

"Don't be so blue, Peter," my mother said sadly. "I want you to have a good time."

"I'm not blue, " I said. "But I'm not having a good time yet either."

* * *

My mother used to be the blue one as I've mentioned. Not me. I didn't realize how unhappy she was at the time, but I do now, remembering the things we did to cheer her up.

In Edinburgh, where we went to school by bus, we'd stop at the tobacco store to buy her a chocolate

bar and then walk down the pebble path to the gate
of the cottage where we lived and she'd be there, all
wrapped up against the bitter, wet cold, only a circle of her face showing, her eyes red from crying or
else from the wind.

"Chocolate," she'd smile, kissing each of us on
top of the head. "I've been waiting all day for you to
come home and bring me chocolate."

Once I asked if she'd been crying.

"Not crying," she said.

"But you seem gloomy."

"It is lonely when you're all at school,"

"And you have no friends because we're always
moving."

"That's true," she said.

She was like I am now, since we've moved to
Boston.

* * *

By the time we had moved to Tokyo to the tiny two-
bedroom apartment, I'd catch my mother sitting in
the kitchen before dinner looking off into the distance, or out of the window, where all we could see

was another steel and glass high-rise apartment and the sky.

What we did to please her in Tokyo was to draw pictures of our family that she taped to the walls — wild pictures in brilliant colors, Tobias purple, our father magenta, Emily periwinkle-blue.

"Now I have my family around all day," my mother laughed as our apartment filled up with crazy pictures of us.

Everywhere that we went, except to school, my mother came too. I thought she wanted always to be with us, but now I suppose she didn't have anything better like law school to do.

After school, we had a ritual drinking of milky tea and eating cookies. My mother and I would sit at the table while the other kids played in the living room and she'd ask me about my day.

"A lot happened," I'd say although one day was pretty much like the next day, at least at school.

"Like what?" She'd put her chin in her hand, open her eyes wide, and listen as if what I had to tell her was the most interesting thing she'd ever heard.

"Well," I'd begin, "Brady fainted in music class and I got to read my composition on Rome and Mr.

Laker said I was very imaginative but needed reins on my dreams, whatever that means. And then . . ." I'd stop to make sure I had her full attention. "Something terrible happened after recess."

"What happened after recess?" she'd ask me breathlessly.

Nothing terrible had happened, of course, but sometimes on my way home from school, I'd make up stories just to please her.

* * *

When my mother came up to the top floor to check on me, I was in bed in the dark but not asleep, wishing I had taken one of those Christmas cookies with red-and-green sprinkles, thinking about Emily and why she wasn't home from school yet.

"Emily has Brownies today and then she's going to Sara's house for dinner," she said when I asked her where Emily had gone.

"I didn't think we were supposed to go to other people's houses on school nights," I said.

"That was last year," my mother said.

I closed my eyes. I could tell I was about to get

the "what's the matter with you and why don't you try to make friends" lecture, and I didn't want to talk about it.

"So I suppose we won't all sleep in the same bed on Christmas Eve like we always have," I said. "Now that we have so many rooms."

"Of course you will," my mother said, running her fingers through my hair. "We're not changing everything, Peter. Not the important things."

"Good," I said, rolling over on my side with Rrrr in my arms.

* * *

On Christmas Eve, my father got off work early and we shopped downtown for presents, walking home after dark. It was a clear, cold night with a thick, flaky snow falling on our faces light as air, and my father had his hand on my shoulder telling me about an experiment he was doing on synapses in the brain. I don't have an aptitude for science and not much interest in it either, but walking along with my father, listening to his warm and serious voice, made me feel grown-up and suddenly very happy.

"Are you liking Eaton any better?" he asked after he'd finished his monologue on the brain.

"I am." I said it to be kind and not upset my father but I actually meant it as well. It was nice to walk down the block toward our house, to see the red-and-white lights shimmering in the windows and hear the sounds of singing in the distance, the church bells ringing, the gradual accumulation of snow.

I was even starting to like Boston, I thought as I followed my father in the front door of our house, and there was Emily, bundled up in her ski jacket and scarf and hat, her eyes red from crying.

"Barbara Frietchie's gone," she said.

"Disappeared," Tobias said.

My mother was in her coat and hat, as well.

"We're going to look around the neighborhood," she said to my father.

"What happened?" I asked, full of accusation.

"Nobody knows," Susanna said.

"We came home tonight and he wasn't here," Tobias said.

"He was here when I got home," my mother said. "And then the postman came with packages from Grandmother, and I'm afraid he may have slipped out the front door."

"I knew this would happen," I said furiously.

"He's my cat," Tobias said, taking my mother's hand. "There's no reason for you to be so bad-tempered."

We walked along Beacon Street, calling, "Kitty, kitty" and "Here Barbara Frietchie, Frietchie, Frietchie." We turned the corner and walked up Walker and then down State, asking people as we passed, going up to houses and knocking on the door, wondering had they seen Barbara Frietchie and would they call us if they did.

We walked through the alleys and peered over the back fences, calling, "Kitty, kitty. Here kitty, kitty, kit."

Nothing.

Once we heard a meow and rushed down the street to the place where the sound had come from, and there on the front steps of someone's house was a snow-white cat with a loud meow, but his owner was not at home so we couldn't ask about Barbara Frietchie.

We walked until the downstairs lights went out

in some of the houses, and people were going to bed. We heard the bells for the evening church services playing "O Come All Ye Faithful."

Finally, we gave up.

Susanna was crying from the cold, and Tobias was crying because of Barbara Frietchie. It was almost nine o'clock and we hadn't eaten dinner.

So we went home and my mother served us some hot potato soup and sandwiches, but no one was hungry.

My father read Dickens's *A Christmas Carol*, trying to pretend it was a perfectly ordinary Christmas Eve, but I could hear the sadness in his voice. We didn't even try to sing Christmas carols.

"He'll find his way home," my father said, when he kissed me goodnight, in my own bed, with Rrrr under the covers.

"Are you sure?" I asked.

"I very much hope he will," he said, but I knew that he wasn't sure at all. "Cats are very smart."

"Barbara Frietchie may be sweet," I said, "but he's easily confused."

For a long time, I lay there thinking of Barbara

Frietchie in the cold, in the snow, a bewildered cat who had never been outside in his life, trying to find his way home on Christmas Eve.

I was wide awake looking at the ceiling when I heard someone on the way up to my room in bare feet.

"Peter?"

It was Tobias.

"It's Christmas Eve."

"I know."

"We're supposed to tell ghost stories," Tobias said. "We always have."

"Climb in," I said, lifting up the covers so Tobias could climb in next to me.

"I think I heard Emily," Tobias said.

I heard her too, heard her calling to Susanna in a loud whisper, and in a moment, they were both standing in my doorway looking in at the darkness.

"Peter?" Emily asked.

"I'm here," I said, moving over in my double bed so there would be room for two more. "Tobias is too."

January

I didn't want to go back to school after Christmas vacation, so I didn't. My mother couldn't figure out what to do about me. My father had gone to Switzerland for a medical conference and she was at home alone with us for two weeks in the middle of her exams at law school.

"I'm not going to school today," I said when I came down on the first day of school after the vacation.

"Are you sick, darling?" she asked me, automatically feeling my head to check for a temperature.

"Nope," I said.

She gave me an odd look.

"Well?" She poured orange juice and gave me a plate of cinnamon toast. "What's up then?"

I shrugged.

"I don't want to go to school."

"I know how you feel," she said, sitting down across from me with her coffee. "Sometimes I wake up in the morning and I can't stand the thought of going to classes."

"That's not exactly what's going on with me." I had given my decision a lot of thought ever since my alarm rang Monday morning.

"What is going on?" she asked.

"I'm *not* going to school." I said it nicely.

"You're not going to school?" she asked and I'm sure she was stalling for time while she thought of what to say to me. She lifted Glimmer onto her lap and finished her coffee, looking out the kitchen window just beyond where I was sitting so she didn't have to look at me directly.

"That's right," I said, feeling confident.

She opened the newspaper folded on the kitchen table and stared at the front page.

"Are the other kids almost ready for school?" she asked, changing the subject.

"I don't know," I said.

"Mmm," she said. "Trouble in Israel again." She looked up. "Well, today after school I thought I'd meet all of you at Laker's for hamburgers."

"That sounds good," I said.

"Since you're not actually sick," she added.

"Right," I said pleasantly.

"And Susanna doesn't have plans this afternoon so could you walk her home?"

"Since I'm not going to school, I probably shouldn't appear perfectly healthy after school," I said.

"This is a final decision?" she asked, getting up from the table.

What I discovered is that my mother couldn't actually *make* me go to school. If I said, which I did, I absolutely won't go, she isn't large enough to carry me there.

It was a strange feeling to realize that I could make my own decisions. Eleven years old isn't that old to decide you're finished with school, and I was exhilarated for the first time since we'd moved to Boston.

"You can make some of your own decisions," she said to me in the refrigerator voice that she saves for the times she is angry at us. "But you're responsible for them."

"No problem," I said.

"I'm not willing to tell the school that you're sick, because you're not."

"What will you tell them?" I asked.

"I'll tell them the truth." She put the dishes in the dishwasher, packed her bookbag with the two-ton law books she carried around, put on her coat and hat and gloves and scarf because it was snowing in Boston as usual. "I'll say that you decided not to go to school today."

"And will you tell them that you couldn't *make* me?" I asked.

"Making you is not my job, Peter," my mother said on the way out the back door.

For a while after she left, I sat at the kitchen table finishing my cereal and wondering if the principal might call to ask why I wasn't at school.

Wondering if anyone in my class would even notice.

I had not made any friends.

"You don't even try to make friends," Emily had said over Christmas vacation when she was asked to birthday parties and sleepovers and lunches and ice skating dates. "You always have this growly face on at school and the kids probably think you don't want friends."

"That's not exactly true," I said although I knew it was.

"That's what Buck's sister said to me when I spent the night," Emily said. "He thinks you don't like him. That you think you're better than he is."

I had watched Buck — who is the kind of guy I would have liked if he'd been at the American School in Tokyo — race through the playground with his friends, or play stickball in the driveway, or hang out on the corner of Beacon and State after school or pass notes back and forth in the library. He didn't seem so anxious to be my friend.

I knew I'd like to *be* friends with some of the

boys in sixth grade. The trouble was I didn't want to work at it. In fact, I didn't know how.

That's what my father said when we went to the movies on New Year's Day.

We were walking to a restaurant after the movie was over, and I was feeling unhappy in the way that movies sometimes make me feel after they've ended, and my father said, "I'm worried about you, Peter." He had his arm around my shoulder in a strong grip. "We've never lived any place long enough for you to make friends, and maybe you don't exactly know how to do it."

"That seems pretty dumb of me," I said. "Like making friends is a big deal."

"It is a big deal," he said.

"Well, the rest of the kids in the family haven't had any trouble," I said.

"It's easier for Susanna because she's young, and maybe Emily hasn't had trouble because girls like to gossip with each other."

"What about Tobias?" I asked. "And he's even got a learning problem."

"He made one friend who helped him to make

others so it hasn't been too hard for him — except the tutoring," my father said.

"I'm just a loser. That's all," I said, shaking his arm from around my shoulder.

"Think about it, General." He hadn't called me General for a long time and it warmed me up to hear the familiar nickname. "Is there anyone in the sixth grade you can imagine as a friend?"

"There's Buck, who's okay," I said. "But he doesn't like me."

"How do you know he doesn't like you?" my father asked.

"There I am every day sitting fourth from the back in the second row, and then going to the library and the playground and the lunchroom, and all the other places he goes. All he needs to do is be my friend. Right?"

"Not exactly," my father said.

"So what do I do?" I asked. "Beg him?"

"Of course not. You just have to let him know that you want to be friends."

"That's lame," I said crossly. "I'd never do anything like that."

At the restaurant, everyone else ordered hamburgers and french fries and chocolate milkshakes. I ordered water and refused to eat, even though I was extremely hungry.

This, I decided on the first day of the New Year, was the bottom of my life. I hated Boston and the cats were dying and my family was breaking up into small separate parts and I had failed at making friends.

I'd starve myself until I disappeared and then they'd certainly be sorry that my life had turned into an empty desert. They would wish they had paid attention before it was too late.

"I'm getting a little tired of your bad mood, Peter," my mother said.

Tobias looked around furtively. I could see the little wheels spinning behind his eyes while he tried to make up his mind whether or not he was going to say something.

"Me too," he said finally. "You've been getting a little mean."

"That's your problem," I said, pushing the water glass across the table.

"I think it's your problem," my mother said, looking at me without a trace of a smile, her blue eyes ice-cold.

I walked home alone. Not exactly alone, but I hung back, half a block from where they were walking, calling for Barbara Frietchie.

"Here kitty, kitty, here kitty, kitty," I called at the top of my voice. I certainly hoped they could hear me through the icy winter air.

Ever since we moved here, Barbara Frietchie had wanted to get out of the front door and look around Boston, and he was a determined cat. Maybe, my father said, he'd found a new family or a girlfriend or taken a subway to Cambridge and was living in Harvard Yard. But we never found him. We put up notices on telephone poles and storefront windows and called the S.P.C.A., which picks up animals off the street. Every day, Tobias and I searched the neighborhood, but no one we spoke to remembered seeing a black-and-white cat who met his description.

Tobias was sad for longer than Susanna had been, but during our Christmas vacation he was invited to go skiing for a weekend and he went and had a wonderful time and probably didn't think once about Barbara Frietchie while he was away.

I guess I was the only one still thinking about him, still wandering through the neighborhood calling his name.

✳ ✳ ✳

I had just gotten up to put my cereal bowl in the dishwasher, wondering what I was going to do all day since the television is broken, when my mother came back in the house.

"Did you forget something?" I asked her.

"In a way," she said sitting down across from me. "I forgot to tell you how upset I've been about Barbara Frietchie."

"Yeah," I said, not in the mood for a heartfelt conversation.

"I know you think it was my fault because he got out the front door when I was supposed to be in charge."

"Not really," I said.

But she was right. I was mad at her about Barbara Frietchie and other things. About moving here and changing into a professional woman instead of being a mother like she used to be. In fact, I was a little mad at everyone in my family, except Rrrr and my father.

"Well, I came back to say I'm very sorry, Peter." She kissed the top of my head, putting her snowy hands on my cheeks. "I know this has been a difficult year — especially for you."

"Thanks," I said.

"And if you reconsider and decide to go to school today, call me in the law library and let me know."

I was wandering around the house with Rrrr over my shoulder, thinking I might get dressed and go downtown if I could find some money, when the telephone rang. It was Buck. I was very surprised to hear from him. Buck had never called me on the phone, and we were not really friends. But I got pretty excited when he said, "This is Buck and I called to tell you about basketball tryouts today and to see if you're sick."

"Sick enough," I said.

I certainly wasn't going to tell him the truth.

"Well, I thought maybe you'd want to try out for the team since you're tall and stuff," he said. "And probably good."

"Maybe," I said. "I hadn't thought about it."

Which wasn't true. I'd been thinking about it ever since I failed to make the soccer team.

I asked if it would be too late to try out tomorrow and he said no, it wouldn't be. Other guys were absent with the flu.

"That's great," I said. "Thanks for calling."

And when I hung up, I picked up Rrrr and danced around the kitchen with him, hopped over the stool, jumped up on the kitchen table, and called my mother at the law library.

"Guess what?" I said.

"Are you all right?" she asked.

"A-okay," I said. "I just wanted to tell you I changed my mind about school, and I'm leaving as soon as I get dressed — in case you call and wonder where I am."

"I'm so glad," she said. "I'll tell the school you'll be coming in."

"Tell them I had a dentist appointment. That's why I'm late."

She laughed. "I don't think I'll tell them that."

"Just say I changed my mind."

I ran upstairs, tripped over Martha Washington, who was sleeping in the middle of the second floor hall, put on my jeans and Celtics shirt, my parka, hat, and gloves, grabbed my bookbag, locked the front door, and ran all the way to Eaton Elementary.

"I thought you were sick," Buck said to me when I sat down in the desk next to him at Social Studies.

"I'm better," I said casually. "I mean, it's boring at home with no one there."

"I know," he said. "I never miss school."

I opened my book on contemporary Latin America and took out my composition assignment.

"Does this mean you're going to try out for basketball?" he asked.

I shrugged.

"Probably," I said. "I haven't played much, but it's worth a try."

"Hey, that's great," Buck said, and he seemed

genuinely pleased, leaning over to Jimbo. "Peter's trying out for basketball."

Jimbo gave me a thumbs-up.

* * *

I walked with Gunner to the tryouts. Buck was already there practicing jump shots with Jimbo and Ethan, who is the tallest boy in the class.

The coach gave me a total of five minutes playing time. I dribbled the ball down the full court three times and got to take a few shots, one of which swished from the foul line.

"Not bad," Buck said afterward when I joined him on the bench.

"Pretty amazing," Ethan said. "You're faster than I thought."

"He's fast," Jimbo said. "Maybe you'll make the first team."

"I don't think so," I said although I was pleased. I doubted that I'd make the first team, maybe the second — but I hadn't been terrible.

When I came back from tryouts to get my books, there was a note on my locker from Emily asking me to meet her after I picked up Susanna. She was sitting on the top step in front of the school when I walked out.

"What's up?" I asked as we went down the front steps of the main building and turned left toward home. "Nothing to do today. No friends?"

"I don't know," Emily said. "It's sort of gloomy in Boston in the winter and all day I've been thinking about Barbara Frietchie and Parsimonious."

"Me too," I said, very pleased and surprised to know that Emily was upset about the cats too.

"Me too," Susanna said softly, taking my hand.

"When I'm with my friends, I don't think about the cats, but today Marianne was sick and Sarah is in the infirmary with the stomach flu and I just wanted to go home to check on Jabberwock."

"I know," I said, throwing my arm around her shoulders in a rush of happiness. "That's exactly how I feel."

✳   ✳   ✳

My mother was home that afternoon, sitting in the kitchen, still in her coat dusted with snow.

"You're home early," I said.

"I finished exams," she said, "and I've been walking around the neighborhood."

My heart leaped up.

"Looking for Barbara Frietchie?"

She nodded.

"Any luck?" I asked.

She folded her arms across her chest.

"No luck," she said. "I followed a snow-white cat on State Street, thinking maybe she'd lead me to Barbara Frietchie, but she disappeared under a house."

Emily flopped down beside my mother, resting against her shoulder.

"Maybe we should have tea and cookies like we used to do," she said. "It's so cold."

"I think that's a very good idea," my mother said, taking off her coat, shaking the snow off her mittens. "Peter, could you make some tea?"

I filled the teakettle with water, turned on the gas, took a bag of gingersnaps out of the cupboard, and sat down with my family, full of a welcome happiness in the disappearing light of late afternoon.

February

I made the basketball team. Not the first team but the second. I was probably the next to last chosen after Ollie Covington since I'm not very good. But I am tall.

On the days that we had practice after school, I stayed later with Ollie Covington and worked on dribbling and defense, but I still didn't hit the basket very often.

Valentine's Day was one of the days I stayed late. When I left, it was quite dark outside and snowing, a kind of silver-glitter snow. The streets were quiet, an eerie sense of gloom in the air.

It's a strange feeling walking in the snow at night, in the soft silence, your face frozen, snow on your eyelashes and in your mouth, the air shimmering as if the world as you know it is no longer real.

I was walking on the third block after Eaton Elementary — our house is nine blocks away — thinking about Valentine's Day.

I hadn't given any valentines. I'm not exactly the type and, besides, I was afraid I wouldn't get any. So I didn't want to embarass myself by writing out thirty-six valentines for everyone in my class and going home with an empty bag. But as it turned out, my bag wasn't empty. It wasn't full either, but there were fourteen valentines, which is okay under the circumstances, and I've read them all. One is from Buck, one from Jimbo, one from Gunner, and one from Ollie. The rest are from the girls in my class who like to talk about sex education.

So I was feeling better than usual and thinking about Valentine's Day and whether we'd have a special dinner with a heart cake, when suddenly through the cold silvery snow shower, I saw Barbara Frietchie.

He was sitting on the top step of a row house

across the street looking very much like himself, only covered with snow. The house, one quite a lot like ours, brown with shutters and a small porch, and which was attached to other houses on either side, was dark except for a porch light and a single light upstairs.

I crossed the street, keeping my eye on Barbara Frietchie. My plan was to stand at the bottom of the steps and call to him. Cats are funny. I wasn't certain he'd be glad to see me, so I didn't want to be too aggressive. A couple of cars went by slowly because of the snow and I waited until they had passed to cross the street, and then I was on the other side looking at the top step where Barbara Frietchie had been sitting, and he was gone.

Somehow, he had disappeared in the time it took for the cars to pass and for me to cross the street.

I called, "Kitty, kitty, here Barbara Frietchie. Here kitty, kitty."

But there was no sign of him.

I went up to the porch, looking over the railings on either side to be sure I hadn't missed him, and then I knocked, peering in the window at the hall. No one came. I knocked again, hard, and called "Is anybody home?" since the doorbell didn't seem to work. But no one came.

* * *

At dinner, my father was home early and my mother had made a valentine cake with white frosting and tiny red cinnamon hearts.

"This is like Tokyo," Susanna said, making a stack of tiny sugar valentines with messages like "Be Mine" and "I Love You." "All of us together and Daddy here and Mommy not doing her homework all night long."

"I liked it when you didn't have anything to do but us," Tobias said to my mother.

"So did I," Susanna said.

"But you're never at home, Susanna," my mother laughed. "You're always on a play-date."

"Still, I like to think you're at home even if I'm away."

"Sometimes I just want to call you and you're at classes," Tobias said.

"But I'm happier now that I have my schoolwork just like you have yours."

"Maybe," Tobias shrugged. "But I'm not."

I was glad that for once someone else was complaining, especially Tobias, because he never complains except about his learning disability.

"I think we're all glad to be settled in our own country and our own house," my father said, but he didn't sound entirely convinced and I sometimes wonder if he isn't like me and likes it better when we travel around the world. But he would never say. He's not that kind of talker.

"Peter isn't glad yet," Emily said, flinging her arm over my shoulder.

"Not yet," I said, but I wasn't unhappy.

I didn't bring up seeing Barbara Frietchie. I'm not sure why. Perhaps I was afraid they wouldn't believe me or maybe, I didn't want them to believe me in case I was mistaken.

Later, after we were in bed, I crept downstairs to Tobias's room, climbed into bed with him and told him what I had seen.

"How do you know it was Barbara Frietchie?" he asked.

"I just know," I said. "He looked exactly like Barbara Frietchie."

Tobias was silent for a moment, and then he asked, "You think he was real?"

"Of course," I said. "A real cat who belonged to you and ran away from home. What do you mean *real?*"

"I mean — a ghost," Tobias said.

"Was the cat I saw a ghost?" I asked.

"That's what I mean."

"No, Tobias. The cat I saw was a cat. Why?"

"Barbara Frietchie could have died and come back as a ghost and that's why he disappeared when you went over to see him," Tobias said. "Ghosts are like that."

"I guess that's true."

We lay there for a while, and then Tobias said, "You think it was Barbara Frietchie."

"I do," I said.

"Then tomorrow we should go to the house where you saw him and find out," Tobias said.

"We'll leave here early so we won't be late for school," I said.

"You don't think he's found a family he likes better than us, do you?"

"No," I said. "I think he couldn't find his way home."

∗ ∗ ∗

In the morning, Tobias and I got dressed quickly, ate breakfast before the girls had come downstairs for school, and headed out, almost running the four blocks to the house where I had seen Barbara Frietchie.

"That one," I said.

"How can you tell? All the houses look the same." Tobias took my hand to cross the street.

"I memorized the house," I said, stopping on the sidewalk in front of it. In Boston, it's still dark early on winter mornings, so the lights in the house were on, even the porch light. The newspaper was still folded at the front door.

Barbara Frietchie wasn't on the top step, and when I looked around I didn't see him, but the lights were on in the house, and I walked up the steps and looked in the window.

"Aren't you going to ring the bell?" Tobias asked.

"I tried. It doesn't work," I said, knocking on the door with my fist until a young man in a suit with his tie around his neck untied came to the door. Behind him was a woman with braids. She was pregnant.

I introduced myself and Tobias and asked them if they had a black-and-white cat with a white bow tie across his black lips. They shook their heads.

"We don't have a cat at all," the man said.

"Well, I saw a cat that I think is our cat sitting on your top step yesterday," I said.

"You did?" the man asked.

He looked back at his wife.

"The only cats that I know of in the neighborhood are Bluesy, next door, and a witchy black cat down the street," the pregnant woman said.

"Our cat's name is Barbara Frietchie," Tobias said. "We lost him on Christmas Eve."

"I'm very sorry about that," the man said kindly, and he took our names and telephone number in case Barbara Frietchie should reappear. "I wish I could be more helpful, but I'm sure I haven't seen a cat like Barbara Frietchie in this neighborhood recently."

And his wife agreed.

✳ ✳ ✳

I walked the rest of the way to school with my hand over Tobias's shoulder. He didn't push it off, but he wasn't very talkative either, until we arrived at the front entrance to Eaton Elementary, and then he turned to me and said with so much sadness I could not forget his voice all day, "I think you saw Barbara Frietchie because you wanted to see him," he said, leaning his head against my jacket. "But he wasn't really there."

"Maybe," I said. "Maybe you're right."

March

In March, after the last basketball game of the season (we won and I scored five points) Buck asked me if I'd like to go skiing with his family in Vermont for spring vacation.

We had gotten to be good friends, Buck and me and Gunner and Jimbo. Sometimes Ollie. I'd spent the night with Buck twice and once with Jimbo, so I suppose it wasn't exactly surprising that he asked me to go to Vermont.

"I get to ask one friend to go skiing with us," Buck said as we walked home after the game. "And you're the friend I choose."

"Thanks," I said. "That sounds great."

"Ask your parents and call me tonight," he said.

"I will," I said with a sinking feeling. "I'm not sure what our plans are so I'll ask and let you know."

The truth is, it didn't sound great at all even though I liked Buck and had a good time at his house on sleepovers. But when he asked me, my stomach rolled over and I broke out in a terrible sweat thinking I might be sick. I don't know why. I just knew I didn't want to go skiing in Vermont with Buck's family. It wasn't personal. I didn't want to go skiing with anybody's family. I said good-bye to Buck and walked the rest of the way home hoping I wouldn't have a heart attack before I got to the front door.

In February, after Barbara Frietchie appeared and disappeared, I had started to leave notes around the house for my mother. I got the idea from a book called *Losing*, which we read in language arts. It was about a boy whose mother has died, and he leaves notes for her in case she comes back to find him. My notes were reminders to my mother about the way our lives used to be before we moved to Boston, and my hope was to bring her back to the person I had known when she was a full-time mother.

"Buy cookies for tea — chocolate chips or Oreos are my favorite. Love, Peter," I'd write on a three-by-five card and tape it on the fridge.

"Toast marshmallows after school in the fireplace. Love, P," I'd write.

"Buy construction paper so we can make family pictures this weekend. Love, P."

"Remember First Pact. Love, Peter." I put that note on the inside of the front door so we could all see it as we left for school.

The morning before my final basketball game, I'd left a note on the kitchen table in green Magic Marker.

"Family Dinner this Monday night," it said.

✳ ✳ ✳

Emily came up the steps of our house just as I was opening the front door.

"Did you win?" she asked.

"Twenty-four to eighteen," I said. "I scored."

She hugged me.

"I was hoping to see the game but they wouldn't let us out of art class," she said. We dropped our bookbags and coats and went into the kitchen where my mother had already started dinner.

"So I hear you scored," she said, kissing the top of my head.

"Five points," I said.

"Amazing," she said.

"I know." I took a handful of chocolate-chip cookies.

Emily had slipped into a chair at the kitchen table and was looking at the note I'd left that morning.

"Are we having a family dinner?" she asked opening her bookbag, taking out her homework.

"This is a family dinner," my mother said, ladling chili into bowls.

"But Susanna and Tobias aren't here," I said.

"Neither is Daddy," Emily added.

"We never have dinner with the whole family on weekdays," I said.

"We're all very busy," my mother said.

"Not me," I said.

"You're very busy, Peter. You just don't notice."

"I notice. I'm more busy because of basketball."

"And you're about to be especially busy," she said, sitting down with us at the table. "Buck's mother called this afternoon to ask if you'd like to go skiing for spring vacation."

It was just Emily and my mother and me, Glimmer under the table with a rubber mouse. Susanna was at a play-date and Tobias was at tutoring.

"Did you know that she was going to call?" she asked.

"Yes, I knew," I answered, suddenly cold all over.

"Well, it's a lovely opportunity for you, darling."

A lovely opportunity was not exactly what I wanted.

"I thought we were going someplace as a family for spring vacation," I said.

"We can't," Emily said.

"I don't have the same vacation as you do and Daddy has a medical conference in London," my mother said.

"I'm going away to visit Plimoth Plantation with MacKenzie," Emily said.

"And I think Tobias may be going on a camping trip with some people in his class," my mother said.

"Great. So it's just me and Susanna at home for a week," I said.

"Not if you go skiing."

"So what did you say to Buck's mother?"

"I told her I thought you'd love to go."

My mother lit the candles on the kitchen table, dimming the lights so I could hardly see the chili.

"You told her what?"

"That you'd love to go," she said.

"You were wrong," I said.

"I thought you'd be thrilled, Peter."

"I'm unthrilled."

"Then I'll have to call Buck's mother back."

"Don't answer for me, Mom, ever in my life again," I said.

"At least you have a friend and aren't so lonely all the time," Emily said.

"Thanks a lot," I said, and I lifted my arm, knocking it hard against my chili bowl so the bowl flew at Emily, spraying chili all over her. "I wasn't lonely, dimwit," I said, and left the table in a hurry to avoid what was certainly going to happen next.

I have been having nightmares. They started after I saw Barbara Frietchie on the top step of the house on State Street. It's actually one nightmare that happens over and over, not every night, but often. In the dream, I am in a small locked room that hasn't got any windows. When the dream begins, even though I've had the same dream a zillion times before, I am not afraid to be alone in the room, although I should be. Across from me is a black-and-white cat who looks very much like Barbara Frietchie. He even has a white bow tie on his black lips. But it isn't Barbara Frietchie. I don't know this for certain, but I have reason to believe it isn't Barbara Frietchie.

The cat is the size of a regular boy cat, not particularly fat, and he is sleeping, curled up, across from me. But as I watch him, thinking to myself, "Is he Barbara Frietchie or not?" he begins to grow. And grow and grow and grow.

I move over to the corner of the room, press myself against the wall. The cat has grown so large, so quickly, that there is no space for me to stand. I'm certain that I'll be squashed or smothered or flattened — any of these. And certainly dead.

In my dream, I can't breathe because of the weight of the expanding cat on my chest and over my face. Every time I have had this dream, I wake up with Rrrr sleeping at the foot of my bed, and I am gasping for breath.

Lately I don't want to go to sleep at night. I am becoming an insomniac. That's the word my father has for not sleeping, and he tells me I'm awfully young to be an insomniac. I've told him about the nightmare and he says he understands, and I'm sure he does understand. But not completely.

My mother brings me hot milk to make me sleepy and rubs my back and plays soft music on the tape recorder, but sometimes nothing works, and I lie in bed in the dark, hoping I won't fall asleep and dream again.

After I threw the bowl of chili at Emily, I ran upstairs, locked my door, put on my pajamas, stuck Rrrr under the covers and turned out my light. I knew my mother was going to be coming upstairs with all of her questions about why I didn't want to go skiing with Buck and his family and why I threw the chili bowl and why I'd been a general "pain in the neck," even though I made the second-string basketball team and have some new friends.

And I can't answer her. I don't know why. Something is still the matter with my life.

A long time passed or it felt like a long time before my mother finally knocked at the bedroom door. I unlocked it and climbed back into bed.

"I should have asked you first if you wanted to go skiing with Buck's family," she said, sitting down on the bed next to me. "I just thought you'd be happy to go."

I didn't answer.

"It sounds as if they have a wonderful time, Peter. They rent a little cabin and ski all day and have supper in the main lodge and hot chocolate around the fire in their cabin."

"Why can't we do that?" I asked. "All of us together."

"Because we can't."

"It's too bad," I said.

"Not *too* bad," my mother said. "Not the worst thing."

I shrugged.

"I don't want to go skiing with Buck's family," I said, my eyes shut tight.

"But he is your friend, isn't he?"

"Of course, he's my friend." I was impatient. "I'm making friends."

"I know you are," she said.

"I'm turning into the normal, almost twelve-year-old boy you were hoping I'd be in Boston," I said putting a pillow over my face. "I just don't want to go skiing. Get it?"

"I understand," my mother said softly.

"No, you don't understand," I said.

"Then maybe you should explain it to me," she said.

I had wondered myself. While I was walking home, down Beacon Street, after Buck had asked me and I had had that terrible sinking feeling, I wondered why I was frightened to leave my family. For that is what it was about.

I was afraid to leave. Not necessarily to go skiing with Buck, although that didn't sound like fun to me. But I was just afraid to walk out of my front door, down the steps, into someone else's car and drive miles and miles away from this place where my family lived with our remaining cats. Just the thought of leaving made me lose my breath.

"I'm afraid of what will happen if I go," I said to my mother.

She was silent for a long time, taking Rrrr on her lap and scratching him between the ears. She folded her legs under her and looked out the window at the darkness striped with street lights.

"So what do you think?" I asked.

"It's not going to Vermont, is it? It's leaving here."

"I feel glued. As if my staying home protects our lives from changing completely."

"I think I do understand, Peter," she said softly. She ran her slender fingers through my hair, leaned over, and kissed me on the forehead. "You are the one who remembers what our lives have been."

"Maybe that's it," I said.

"If you have one of those terrible dreams again, wake me up," she said.

But I couldn't sleep. I waited until it was quiet downstairs, and I knew that Emily and Tobias and

Susanna were in bed, probably sleeping, and my mother was in the kitchen sitting with my father while he ate.

Then I crept down the steps. Glimmer and Martha Washington were lying on my parents' bed, back to back, as they sometimes like to do, not wishing to speak to each other personally, but glad to be together, I suppose. I picked them up, carried them to my room, put them at the foot of the bed, and closed the door.

I went back downstairs. Next to Emily, Jabberwock was wide awake, licking her long, yellow chest hairs. Emily was sleeping. Carefully I tiptoed across the room, staying on the rug, and lifted Jabberwock, who gave a soft meow. Emily stirred and I stopped, but she didn't wake up, so I tiptoed back across the room with Jabberwock in my arms. I went up the steps, into my room, put Jabberwock at the foot of the bed with Glimmer and Martha Washington, locked the door to my bedroom, slipped into bed next to Rrrr, and turned off my light.

April

*

It was probably a good thing. By April, I was
pretty busy. I made first string on the softball team,

Lately, the cats were always together. I began to
notice it after the night they all slept with me in
my room. The next day when I came home from
school, the four of them were squashed together on
the window seat in the living room facing the back
garden. Rrrr didn't come over to greet me as he usually did when I came home from school. He lifted
his head, gave me a look of boredom, and then nuz-
zled into the backside of Martha Washington and
went to sleep.

It was probably a good thing. By April, I was
pretty busy. I made first string on the softball team,

playing second base, and had practice every afternoon unless the weather was bad. I was still friends
with Buck. I didn't go skiing with his family on
spring vacation, but already by the middle of April,
I'd had three more sleepovers at his house, and he'd
come twice to mine. Only the second night, he had
to call his father to pick him up because he's aller-
gic to cats.

Sometimes I didn't get home until after six,
later than the rest of the kids, except for poor
Tobias, who still had tutoring. Those days, I'd come
in the house and my mother would be in the
kitchen cooking dinner, talking with Susanna and
Emily and Tobias, if he was home, and the cats
would be lying together under the kitchen table. It
made me feel important to be arriving late, with so
many things on my mind — softball and homework and research on South Africa in the library
and meeting Buck at the drugstore. I even had a sort
of girlfriend, who liked me better than I liked her,
but she did give me a very good softball for my
birthday, which was almost worth the trouble of
having her call every night.

I'd walk into the kitchen, pick up Rrrr, sit down at the kitchen table and take over the conversation, telling everyone about my day, as if they'd been waiting for me to come home to tell them about it.

"You have so many friends now," Emily said one afternoon.

"I have fourteen," Susanna said. "Peter doesn't have that many."

"It's wonderful, Peter," my mother said.

"I don't know if I like it as much as when you were home first, before me," Emily said.

"You're the one who kept telling me to get a friend and stop moping around, feeling sorry for myself," I said.

"But I meant one or two friends like me. I didn't think you'd get so many. It's like you've forgotten us — your family, your brother and sisters," she said. "And the cats. You don't even worry about the cats any longer."

"Of course I worry about them," I said defensively.

But Emily was right. Since it was spring and baseball season, I hardly ever thought about the cats any longer, at least in the way I had thought about them after we moved to Boston and Parsimonious had died.

That night, in bed with my light off, still too worried about nightmares to sleep easily, I thought about what Emily said. Rrrr was at the foot of my bed, purring louder than usual, and I pulled him up beside me, listening for my mother, hoping she would come up soon to kiss me goodnight.

I must have dozed off. When I woke up with a start, there was a lot of commotion downstairs on Emily and Tobias's floor and I ran down to see what was the matter. I didn't even notice that Rrrr wasn't on my bed, although I thought about it later. Never, ever since I can remember, has Rrrr left my room after I've gone to bed.

Emily was standing on her bed with Susanna, holding an unhappy Jabberwock, and Susanna was crying. Tobias and my mother were looking at something on the floor near the foot of Emily's bed.

What I saw as I ran down the steps was a stripey tail, and, of course, my first guess was that something had happened to Rrrr.

Which was true in a way.

As I got to the door to Emily's bedroom, my mother held up her hand for me not to come any nearer.

"Rrrr has a rat," Emily said.

"Yuck." Susanna squeezed her eyes shut and held herself.

"Dead?"

"No," Tobias said. "Alive. In his mouth."

The beige rug in Emily's room was stained with rat blood, and Rrrr lay on the rug, his teeth around the rat's neck, his paws holding the body of the scrambling rat. There was a low growl I'd never heard before coming from somewhere in his throat.

"What are you going to do?" I asked my mother, trying to appear calm, although I wasn't.

"I don't know what to do, Peter." She looked at me bewildered. "I'd try to kill it but I'm afraid I can't do anything without hurting Rrrr."

"Don't hurt Rrrr," I said, trying to think of the best thing to do.

"I'll try," Tobias said.

Tobias is not usually very brave — not at all

chicken, just not aggressive. But it's surprising what a person can do in an emergency, and that's what Tobias did.

I don't know how he did it. No one does. Not even Tobias.

He took one of my father's hiking boots and hit the rat. Why the boot didn't hit Rrrr as well is a mystery. But it didn't.

And then there was a dead rat lying in the middle of the rug.

Rrrr, still making that terrible growling sound, wanted to take the rat away with him. But my mother picked Rrrr up, and Tobias put the dead rat in a green garbage bag, and I just stood there amazed and feeling sick, I have to admit.

* * *

We took the rat to the animal emergency room for an autopsy to see if it had any terrible diseases and left Rrrr there for observation to see if he'd been exposed to anything. Then we came home and all of us slept in my mother's bed because we couldn't stand to sleep alone.

"Tell me how it happened." I asked my mother when she turned out the light in her room.

"Rrrr flew down the steps from your floor chasing the rat," my mother said. "So my guess is that he was sleeping in your bed as usual and the rat must have come from somewhere — I'll get the exterminators tomorrow — and he chased it down the steps to my floor and then down the next set of steps and into Emily's room, where he caught it."

"Yuck," Susanna said.

"And that's when you came downstairs," my mother said to me.

"So Rrrr sort of saved your life," Emily said.

"We don't know that Peter's life was in danger," my mother said. "But Rrrr certainly had in mind protecting him."

"See," Emily said.

"I hated tonight," Susanna said.

"Except Tobias was brave," I said.

"Tobias was very brave," my mother said.

"Do you think Rrrr's going to be all right?" I asked.

"I'm sure he is," my mother said.

"It'll be icky to sleep with him, though, with rat all over his mouth," Susanna said.

"They'll clean his mouth at the animal emergency room," my mother said, and kissed each of us goodnight.

"Do you remember what you used to sing in Houston when we walked to school?" I asked.

"Of course," my mother said. "I dreamed I was in rat's alley," and we all chimed in laughing. "Where the dead men lost their bones."

✳   ✳   ✳

For a long time, I lay there listening to the others' breathing, unable to sleep.

"Emily?" I said, after a while, hoping she was still awake.

"Yes?"

"I feel bad about forgetting the cats," I said. Somehow I felt responsible for the arrival of the rat in our lives. "I won't forget them any longer."

"That's okay," she said. "You remembered everything for a long time."

Rrrr turned out to be fine — and so did the rat, although he was dead. The exterminators came and got rid of a family of rats that lived in the attic part of our house next to my bedroom, and by the next afternoon when I came home from school, the first one home that day, the cats were squashed together as usual, sleeping in the window seat facing the garden.

May

I was still sitting in my bedroom on my bunk bed when I heard the front door open and thought I heard my father call, "Anybody home?"

I went down the first flight of stairs.

"Gail?"

"It's me," I called. "I got out of softball early."

It was my father.

He must have gotten home earlier than he had planned.

I couldn't see him but I heard him say something that I didn't understand. I guessed that he had seen Rrrr under the hall table.

I went down the second flight of stairs to the floor where Emily and Tobias's rooms are and listened. I tried to look down the stairwell but I couldn't see Rrrr. I did see my father. He was standing in the hall holding his suitcase, just standing there without moving.

"Did you hear me?" I called.

"I heard you, Peter," he said in his low, comfortable voice. "I'll be right up."

"I can't come downstairs," I said.

"I know."

I was sitting at the foot of Tobias's bed when my father came upstairs, sat down on the bed beside me, put his arm tight around my shoulders, and kissed the top of my head.

"Do you think it was a rat disease?" I asked.

"No, I know it wasn't the rat, Peter," he said.

"He just died. He was fine this morning when I left for school."

"He didn't just die out of the blue. He had some kidney problems."

"You never told me," I said.

"When he went to the vet, the doctor told us

that he could live a long time or a short time. There was no way of telling."

"You didn't want to worry me, is that right?"

"There was nothing we could do. His kidneys failed."

"I feel terrible," I said.

"I know you do," he answered. "So do I. Rrrr has been a noble cat."

"The best," I said.

✳ ✳ ✳

That night, before dark, we had a funeral in the back garden, and buried Rrrr in a towel. Tobias and I dug a deep hole and we put Rrrr in and covered him with dirt and made a cross out of sticks. He was buried next to Parsimonious. I gave a speech without crying, saying what a fine cat he had been and how I'd never know another cat so good. We sang "O, God our help in ages past," although my father requested a livelier song. Emily said a prayer and Susanna said she could see Rrrr flying on silver wings in the sky, even though it was almost dark.

Then we went inside and got ready for bed, and our father read to us in my bedroom. He let us all sleep together: Emily and Susanna, Tobias and me.

"Too much has changed this year," I said when he kissed me goodnight.

"A lot has changed, I know," he said.

I liked that he simply agreed with me and didn't try to make things seem fine when they weren't.

Tobias lay very still next to me, but I could tell that he couldn't get to sleep, and I could hear Emily and Susanna whispering in the bottom bunk.

"Are you awake, Peter?" Emily asked finally.

"I can't get to sleep," I said.

"Me neither," Emily said.

"Are the rats still in the attic?" Susanna asked.

"They were exterminated," I said.

"Dead?" Susanna asked.

"No, just put in bags and taken away," I said.

"I don't want to talk about rats," Tobias said.

And just when he said that, a strange light slid through the pane glass of my bedroom window. Emily saw it too. I sat up and slid down to the floor.

Where the light had been, which was gone by

the time I got to the floor, was Barbara Frietchie. I saw him absolutely clearly. He was standing in the corner of my room, facing me, with his white bow tie lips. I guess I made a funny sound, because Tobias sat up in bed.

"Peter," he said in a breathless voice. "Do you see what I see?"

Emily climbed out of bed, with Susanna wrapped around her waist and stood next to me.

"It is Barbara Frietchie."

"Don't move," I said. "We should be very still."

Barbara Frietchie walked across the room to the opposite corner where my desk is and stuck his nose under the desk as if he had discovered something there, and when he raised his head, Parsimonious slunk out from under the desk, lay on her side, and licked the white fur on her belly.

Tobias had climbed down from the top bunk and we were all four huddled together on the bottom bunk, whispering.

"We can't scare them. We have to be really quiet," I said.

"Are they real?" Susanna asked.

"Ghosts," Tobias said.

"Do they know we're here?" Emily asked.

"I think they know or they wouldn't have come here," I said. "They could have gone anyplace."

"So they wanted to see us," Tobias said.

"Of course," I said. "We're their family."

"I know," Susanna said. "I can tell Parsimonious is so glad to see me."

"I wonder if Rrrr will come," Emily asked.

"Maybe he hasn't been dead for long enough to come," I said.

"It feels as if he's already here on the bed where he was sleeping just last night." Susanna reached down to the bottom of the bunk bed. "It's still warm."

And Rrrr *was* there. Just where he always slept, his head curled under his paw, his tail wrapped around him, his ears up.

I reached out to touch him. It was automatic. I didn't even realize I was doing it until Tobias said "stop" and by the time he had said it and I had pulled my hand back, Rrrr was gone.

As soon as Rrrr disappeared, we looked over at

the desk to the place where Barbara Frietchie and Parsimonious had been, and they were gone too.

"Now we'll never see them again." Susanna was crying. "And it's your fault, Peter."

"But they came once," I said. "And so they'll come again."

"How do you know?" Susanna asked.

"He just does," Tobias said.

"I know too," Emily said quietly.

* * *

We didn't sleep very well that night, all of us squashed together with the remaining cats on the bottom bunk, but the next morning I felt different than I had in a very long time, since we moved to Boston last August.

"Do you believe in ghosts?" Tobias asked me as we got ready for school.

"I do," I said.

"I mean, really believe in them?"

"Completely," I said.

"You think they were real cats?" Susanna asked.

"I think they were ghost cats," I said, picking up Martha Washington and Glimmer. Emily carried Jabberwock and we all went downstairs to breakfast where my parents were waiting for us.

"Did you sleep well?" my mother asked.

"Great," Susanna said.

"Fine," I said.

"No nightmares?" my father asked.

"None at all," I said, and warmed by the early spring sun coming through the window, we slid into our chairs at the kitchen table, side by side for a single moment before we rushed out the back door with our bookbags on our way to school.

About This Scholastic Signature Author

SUSAN SHREVE "has a spectacular gift for taking ordinary youngsters and making them do extraordinary things" (*The Philadelphia Enquirer*). Her novels for children and adults include *Jonah, the Whale and How He Became Incredibly Famous*; *The Flunking of Joshua T. Bates*; *The Gift of the Girl Who Couldn't Hear*; and *The Visiting Physician*. She is a professor of English at George Mason University in Washington, D.C.